COMMON

The Lora Fletcher Chronicles

Book 1

Andrea Irving

e-book:

ISBN-10 0-9979950-2-5

ISBN-13 978-0-9979950-2-2

Paperback:

ISBN-10 0-9979950-3-3

ISBN-13 978-0-9979950-3-9

To Whitney. Because, you know, Nestea Raspberry Iced Tea, Chex Mix, and purple grapes.

Table of Contents

MAP

CHAPTER 1

CHAPTER 2

CHAPTER 3

CHAPTER 4

CHAPTER 5

CHAPTER 6

CHAPTER 7

CHAPTER 8

CHAPTER 9

CHAPTER 10

CHAPTER 11

CHAPTER 12

CHAPTER 13

CHAPTER 14

CHAPTER 15

CHAPTER 16

CHAPTER 17

CHAPTER 18

CHAPTER 19

CHAPTER 20

CHAPTER 21

CHAPTER 22

CHAPTER 23

CHAPTER 24

CHAPTER 25

Map

ERASTEEN

YDRIS

Mount Rathbone

Windy Heath

Blackmoor

Grey Falls

Haven dale

Horn Peak

Green Meadows

Forest Glen

BORDER RANGE

Round Lake

Glimmen

KORLISSE

RIVER YDRIS

High Hill

Lone Pine

James Lake

Long Lake

Azure Shores

Rock Harbor

ANOURIA ↓

Arbor Cove

SHAAD →

CHAPTER 1

Lora tucked a lock of dirty, tangled, mousy brown hair behind her ear and leaned closer to the door. She had to be quiet if she was going to eavesdrop without anyone catching her. She wasn't in her own house, which threw her normal stealth totally off. She knew they were talking about her. Why else would her father drag her to the keep? She hoped she wasn't in trouble for setting the neighbor's thatching on fire. It was just an accident, after all.

She picked at her fingernails and tore off part of one. Since its edge was sharp, she stuck it in her mouth and bit it the rest of the way off, taking care not to bite it so short that it bled. She was always biting her nails too short. The door began to open, and she started, ripping the nail too short anyway.

She jumped back across the hall and tried to stand as still as she could with her sore finger in her mouth. The voices she could hear through the door grew louder. It seemed her father, Mark Fletcher, maker of all the arrows in Haven Dale, was talking to Lord Allistair.

Lord Allistair of Haven Dale was young. Maybe twenty-five at most. He had hazel eyes and wavy black hair that he kept short. All of the girls in town thought him very dashing. He had a reputation as a bit of a scoundrel because so many young girls liked him so well. He had a younger sister, Tiana, who was about to be married. She was a little stuck up, so none of the town girls had anything nice to say about her.

"Is this her?" Lord Allistair asked as he stepped out of his study. He frowned as he took in her appearance.

Mark Fletcher nodded. "Yes, milord."

Lord Allistair's frown deepened. "She doesn't look much like you, Fletcher. She's twelve, you say? Awfully skinny and... dirty." He sighed. "Can you read and write?" he asked Lora. When she nodded, he continued, "Ride?"

"Yes, and I can shoot too," she told him, her finger still in her mouth.

The young lord grimaced. "What about embroidery or dancing?" When she shook her head, he muttered an oath under his breath. "We'll have to gentle her up before she goes to the capital. She has to have training as a wielder or else she'll burn down the village. But since only nobles ever go to train for that, we have to be able to pass her off as one." He crossed his arms in front of his chest. "We have our work cut out for us." He turned to Lora's father. "That will be all. You are dismissed."

"Her clothing and personal things are at our home," Mark stuttered. "I didn't expect you to take her right now."

Allistair waved him off. "Nothing she currently has will be appropriate. You can send a stuffed toy or whatever she wants later. We need to get started immediately, so we can prevent any more accidents. Your indenture begins tomorrow, Fletcher." He turned on his heel, beckoned to Lora to follow him, and he strode down the hall.

Lora quickly hugged her father and gave him a kiss. She had no idea what was going on, but she knew she could not disobey his lordship. She ran after him as swiftly as she could.

He stopped when he heard her behind him. "First lesson," he said. "Walk. Do not run. A lady never runs." When she opened her mouth to explain, he held up his hand. "Second lesson, no back talking. What are you called again?"

"Lora, milord," she replied.

"No, no. that won't do." He tapped his chin with his fingers. "That's much too common. If you are to be my ward, you'll need something a little bit more genteel." He continued tapping his fingers. "Lorana. Lorana of Haven Dale. Similar enough to Lora for you to quickly get used to responding to it and different enough to rise you above the other village girls."

She frowned. Her father had told her she'd been named after her grandmother. She didn't like not honoring her memory. But lesson number two was no back talking...

"I'm taking you to my sister now," he told her. He held out his arm for her, and when she grabbed it, he winced. "You'll be in her charge. She will teach you about being a lady. I hope to get you to Glimmen in two sevendays, so young Lorana, learn fast."

"Yes, milord," she replied.

He shook his head. "That won't do at all," he said. "We'll have to pass you off as a distant relative. So you'll call me Cousin Allistair. We're relations on my father's side." He paused and glanced at her out the corner of his eye. "Very distant."

Lora blinked. "Of course, Cousin Allistair."

"At least you learned that quickly, young Lorana." He cleared his throat as they came to a doorway. The walls of the keep were rough stone covered with old tapestries. Most of the doors were ancient oak and looked more utilitarian than anything else. This one was painted white. The hinges looked to be made of metallic ribbons, rather than leather straps or strong metal bars. There were carvings of symbols and scenes all over it. He knocked twice and a feminine voice beckoned. "The women's room," he explained. "You'll spend most of your time in here while you are with us."

She stared at the door and swallowed. "I understand," she said.

Allistair tapped his foot while they waited. After a moment, a young woman in plain clothes opened the door. "Maisie, I need my sister." When the girl turned around, he continued, "Maisie is Tiana's lady's maid. She will be assisting you, as well."

"Come in, Allistair," Tiana called. She frowned when she took in Lora's appearance. "Good gracious! What's this?"

"This is Lora, the fletcher's daughter," he replied as he led her across the room. "She has some magic and I've agreed to have her educated in Glimmen as a wielder. Evidently she's set several things on fire, so the education is for everyone's benefit. Mark Fletcher will be paying for her education with a ten-year indenture to me. From here on out, she will be Lorana, our distant cousin on our father's side. It would be too difficult to get her educated as a commoner. I require your assistance in getting her ready for society. You have two sevendays. I expect her to be dressed and ready for dinner tonight."

He unwound Lora's arm from his and let go of it. He bowed to them and left.

Tiana looked very appraisingly at her charge. "Maisie, run to the village and bring back the tailor with some ready-made pieces. She'll need several things for every day, as well as something for special occasions. Have your sister draw a bath in the chamber next to mine." Maisie curtsied and left the room. "Can you read?"

Lora nodded. "I can read, write, and do sums," she explained. "I can shoot and ride, but I can't dance or do any fancy sewing." She looked down at her feet, stuck a lock of hair in her mouth, and began to chew on it.

"Take your hair out of your mouth and look up at me," Tiana said. Her voice was stern, but not mean. "If you're to be a wielder, you should look into people's eyes as an equal." She paused and tucked a stray lock of her glossy, dark brown hair behind her ear. "Etiquette, protocol, and ladies' pursuits are what we'll concentrate on. How well do you read? What kind of sums can you do?" She gestured for Lora to sit and winced when she flopped onto the chaise.

"Like this," she said. Tiana walked gracefully over to an overstuffed chair and slowly lowered herself onto the seat taking care to keep her back straight. She placed her hands in her lap after gently arranging her skirts.

"I can read the school primer," she replied. Lora sat up straight and tucked her hands in between her knees. "I keep track of the funds for the orders in father's shop." She had sagged into a slouch by the time she was finished speaking.

Tiana rose, walked to a bookshelf, selected two volumes, and walked back. She handed the smaller volume to Lora. "Read to me," she said as she placed the other book atop Lora's head. "Read to me and keep this book from falling off." She let go and the book slid to Lora's lap. Tiana replaced it.

After several awkward movements and replacing the book onto her head as many times as she moved, Lora finally managed to balance it for more than a second. She opened the smaller book and held it in front of her only to have the larger book slide onto her lap. She replaced it, opened the smaller book again, and the large book dropped behind her. After nearly an hour, she managed to look at the first page.

"Well?" Tiana asked. "Do you know it?"

"Most of the words," Lora said. "I can guess at the rest. I know this story." She turned to look at Tiana, and she lost the book again.

Tiana hid a smile behind her hand. She had to give Lora credit for trying. She'd be nowhere near society-ready in two sevendays, but she'd definitely pass for a poor relation. "Good. Once you can consistently sit with the book on your head while reading from a book, we'll start walking with the book on your head."

Lora's eyes filled with tears. It was all too much to take in. "If you say so... Cousin Tiana."

After another hour or so of continued tears and practice with the books, Maisie returned with the tailor. The tailor, whom Lora had known her whole life, shook her head at the whole situation. "I've brought the dresses, milady. I've also brought things to help her hair and nails." She'd known Lora from infancy and was well aware of her flaws and habits.

"Indeed," Tiana said, failing to conceal a yawn.

The tailor laid out five dresses, three night gowns, and several changes of underthings. There were four dresses for every day, which were nicer than anything Lora had owned up until then, and one fancier dress which terrified her. She knew she would feel and act awkwardly once she put it on. She had already discerned she was doing all of the wrong things. Wearing the dress would just make it more obvious that she didn't belong.

"Sit here, Lora, and let me look at your hair," the tailor told her.

Tiana shook her head. "You will address her as Lorana, or Miss Lorana. I know you know her from the village, but she is going to Glimmen as a lady. She will need to get used to being addressed as one."

"Yes, milady," the tailor replied. She beckoned to the frightened girl, and when she sat down, she began to comb the snarls out of her hair. "It looks like it will need a trim," she said as she removed her shears from her skirt pocket. "It was cut pretty uneven before, so I'll have to even it out and get rid of the ends she's chewed." She turned Lora's head so it was at the angle she needed, and she began cutting. "I'll have to file all of her nails down too. If I remember correctly, Lor—Miss Lorana likes to bite them."

"I had noticed," Tiana agreed. "Lorana, if I notice, everyone else will notice. You will have to stop chewing your hair and nails. You'll need to develop a habit less harmful to your appearance. If you're anxious about something, count to ten or one hundred. Don't bite your nails. Don't chew your hair. Your hair is an unfortunate color to begin with, and you don't want to draw the wrong kind of attention to it."

The tailor made one final cut and pronounced her task complete. "It still goes down past her shoulders, so she'll be able to braid it. She's too young to wear it up, but she could if she needed to." She turned to Lora. "Get undressed. I need to see if these dresses fit you properly. If we're trying to pass you off as a lady, you can't have ill-fitting gowns, ready-made or not."

Lora blinked back more tears and sniffled miserably. She was embarrassed to shrug out of her clothes in front of these three women, but she did as she was told. She figured doing what she was told was rule number three. When she hesitated at her underthings, Tiana crossed her arms in front of her chest and began to tap her foot. Lora sighed and finished disrobing.

When the tailor handed her some underthings, Tiana shook her head. "Not very tall, scrawny, and no sign of breasts or hips anywhere. Have you begun your monthly courses?" When Lora shook her head, she continued, "I'm sure you will soon. Do you know what it means when that happens?"

"It means I can have children," Lora replied as she pulled on her chemise and underpants. "The baker's wife told me."

"It means that any idiot young man can put a bastard in your belly if you let him put his hands on you," Tiana said bluntly. "My brother is not sponsoring you so you can come home pregnant. Relations are for the marriage bed."

Lora pulled on a dark green dress. It fit her. "I understand, Cousin Tiana." She knew it wouldn't do to contradict Lady Tiana, but no boys ever paid any attention to her. She took the warning for what it was, but knew it wasn't something she needed to worry about.

"Good. I hate to have you keep that gown on while you obviously need a bath, but that other garment you were wearing needs to be burned," Tiana said. "You can bathe later."

The tailor quickly filed down Lora's nails and left, shooting her a look of sympathy as she walked out the door. Lora swallowed back the tears she had just fought off.

Tiana's face softened. "I can't imagine what you're feeling right now. It's a lot of change. You miss your father, but he wanted this for you. Do him proud." When Lora nodded, she continued, "I'll come check on you periodically once you're settled at the Academy.

My betrothed has a town home in Glimmen, so we shall be there

often. That way I can make sure you have clothes as you outgrow

these, bring you letters from your father, teach you about becoming a

woman when the time is appropriate, and retain the illusion of our

relationship. Alright now, enough. Back to work. We have a lot to do."

CHAPTER 2

Lora's progress slowly improved over the next two sevendays. She was attempting to walk across the room, as well as embroider, with the book on her head. She had mostly mastered keeping it there while she read, so Tiana had deemed it necessary to move ahead. Once her ineptitude at embroidery was discovered, she was made to practice with kitchen rags that were to be discarded and bits of thread that were bound for the waste bin. She excelled at her sums, but her reading continued to lag behind. Her riding was passable, but she struggled on the dance floor.

On the day before they were to travel to Glimmen, Tiana threw up her hands in despair. "Gods help us," she declared. "I have no idea what they'll think of you, Cousin. I just hope it doesn't reflect badly on me."

Lora bit her lip. "I'm sorry, Cousin Tiana." Her eyes were red rimmed, but no tears appeared. She was all cried out.

Tiana's gaze softened, as it usually did when Lora tried hard not to cry. "You've had two sevendays to learn what it takes a lifetime for other young ladies your age. It was hopeless from the start, but you've done well. You'll be able to take the lead from the other young ladies at the Academy, and I reiterate that you and I will see each other often. I expect you to dine with us on your free days when we are in town."

She nodded. This was nothing new. Lora knew Tiana was distracted with her upcoming wedding and that it was a huge imposition for her to be given the task of training her to be a lady when so many things needed to be done. "I appreciate your help, Cousin Tiana. I am grateful for everything you and your brother are doing."

"Thank your father, too." Tiana gestured for her to leave. "Go up to your room. You need your rest. We leave early."

The walk to her room was long, and the subject of her father weighed on her mind as it did every night when she made this journey. Lora was very uncomfortable with her father's sacrifice. A ten-year indenture was no small thing. Her father would essentially be working for free with no way to make any additional income unless everything Lord Allistair ordered was finished first. She assumed her brother's duties would increase to make up the difference, and it pained her to know the hardship she was causing.

Still, there was nothing to be done about it. Lora knew very well that not having control of her powers endangered everyone around her. She had set fire to the curtains in the women's room just the day before and knocked over a vase with a gust of air in her distress over her actions. She hoped she could just learn the basics and come home quickly, so her father wouldn't need to pay so much. She knew the odds of that were slim, but she still held to hope.

CHAPTER 3

The journey to Glimmen was long. It took ten days in the carriage, and every waking moment was spent training Lora for life at the Academy. By the time they arrived, her fingers were raw from continually stabbing them with her needle, and she feared her eyes would cross permanently from reading on the bumpy roads. Her neck ached from trying vainly to keep that stupid book on her head. Tiana and she were both very cross by the time the city appeared.

As a commoner, Lora never had occasion to travel outside of Haven Dale. Haven Dale was a sleepy village of about three thousand people. In a village of that size, the daughter of a shop owner could recognize most people by sight, if not by name. The most people she had ever seen in one place at one time was on feast days when they all crowded into the village square for food and dancing.

Glimmen was a city more than one hundred times the size of Haven Dale. Lora's face was pressed up against the carriage's window from the moment the city became visible and nothing a scowling Tiana said could do anything about it. Lora was entranced by everything she saw. Players, which came to Haven Dale but once a year or so, performed on nearly every street corner. Street vendors, unheard of in her village, shouted their wares over the din. The market seemed larger than the whole of Haven Dale. And the noise! And the smells! She was overwhelmed in all of her senses.

"Sit properly, Cousin Lorana," Tiana scolded again. "Come away from the window. I don't care how much of a country bumpkin you are. I will not have you embarrass me with such behavior. You've gotten your nose print and gods know what else all over that window."

"I'm sorry," Lora said, prying herself away from the scenery around her. "I never imagined what the city would be like. It's overwhelming."

Tiana raised an eyebrow. "It's fortunate you will not be going out in it to explore until your third or fourth year at the Academy. You'd be taken advantage of in moments." When Lora's face betrayed her confusion, she continued, "Thieves. Murderers. Rapists. Mostly thieves, but you have to be on your guard. You'll receive some pocket money, and I won't feel sorry for you when you cry to me that it was stolen."

Lora blinked. There was some small thievery where she came from, but nothing like what Tiana described. "I will remember that."

The rest of the ride through the city passed in silence. Lora felt her palms start to sweat once the carriage stopped, and she was glad when Tiana didn't correct her when she wiped them on her skirts. She took the footman's offered hand rather than jumping down as she would have at home, and looked around her trying very hard not to gape at her surroundings.

The Academy was a sprawling complex of buildings, most of which were three to four stories tall. Lora knew that the buildings surrounded a practice yard for the swordsplayers and swordwielders, as well as extensive stables and training grounds for various other purposes. She was not prepared for the immensity of it when she stepped out of the carriage. Her mouth fell open and she instinctively began to pick at her fingernails.

Tiana drew Lora's hands apart. "I'll not have you destroying your nails on your first day here," she said in a low voice. "And close your mouth. You look like some kind of village dullard." When Lora complied, she motioned toward the imposing front entrance with her head. "This way, Cousin. They're expecting us."

Lora swallowed and fell in step behind Tiana. Her fingers twitched with the desire to tear her nails to shreds and then stuff her mouth full of hair to ruin the cut the village tailor had given her. She entered the Academy with her hands in fists at her sides. She knew a lady would have them gently clasped in front of her, but she figured this was better than chewing her nails or hair.

"Lady Tiana," a middle aged man called to her as he descended the stairs. He took her hand and kissed it.

Tiana smiled when she took back her hand and gave a small curtsy, such as one gives an equal. "Lord Everett," she replied with a smile. "May I present my cousin, Lorana?" She turned and gestured to her charge whose mouth had fallen open again as she gaped at her surroundings. Tiana's look darkened. "You'll forgive her, Lord Everett. She is not accustomed to the city."

Lord Everett laughed at Lora's blush. "Of course not," he said. "I will take her to Lady Demetria. She will ensure that Miss Lorana is settled. I am sure that you are busy with preparations for your wedding, so I won't detain you."

Lora's eyes widened even further. This parting was nearly as quick as her parting from her father. She looked at Tiana, who smiled indulgently.

"You will be fine, Cousin Lorana. I will come to see you soon." Tiana patted her on the cheek.

"Goodbye, Cousin Tiana," Lora whispered to Tiana's retreating form. She swallowed once her guardian disappeared out the door and let her gaze fall on Lord Everett.

Lord Everett smoothed back his greying hair and offered her his arm. When she took it, he smiled and began walking. "Miss Lorana, we have one stop before Lady Demetria meets us. It's customary for all new wielder students and won't take but a moment."

Lora was not sure what to say. It wasn't as if she could object. "Of course," she told him as he led her outside.

"Our armory is quite extensive," he said. "You'll need a dagger while you are here. All students learn some measure of self-defense. You will not always be able to rely on your powers, and a quick thrust with a dagger from a skilled fighter will put most threats to rest in time for you to regain your wits and use your powers."

"Of course," she repeated.

They reached the armory after a few minutes and Lord Everett paused after they entered. His gaze fell upon her and he appeared to assess her for a moment before moving on. "Our head armorer is named Blaine. He will find you a suitable weapon."

"I prefer the bow," Lora blurted out.

"Your forest background betrays you, young Lorana," Lord Everett told her. "The bow is a fine choice for you, but it will not help you in close quarters. Ah—here he is. Master Blaine, this is Miss

Lorana. She's just arrived from Haven Dale to begin her training as a

wielder."

Blaine grunted and turned to a wall from which a multitude of

daggers hung. Evidently this request was commonplace, for he

returned with a small dagger and handed it to her without a word.

When Lora took it, she did not notice the two men scrutinizing

her. She looked the knife over, and it appeared sound. She knew next

to nothing about such things and hoped he wasn't testing her on

something she'd neglected to learn in her crash course on being a

noble.

"Well, well, well," Lord Everett said as he crossed his arms in

front of his chest. Blaine grunted and turned back to his work,

seemingly unaffected by whatever piqued Lord Everett's interest. He

held his hand out for the dagger. "If you would, Miss Lorana." When

she handed it to him, he took a deep breath. "This certainly changes

things." He paused and bent down to Lora's level. "This little dagger in your hand," he said as he gestured with it, "makes you a swordwielder."

Lord Everett paused for effect, and he raised his eyebrows when Lora's look remained blank. "Please tell me you know what I am talking about." When Lora continued to stare, he muttered something about country bumpkins under his breath and then cleared his throat. "Wielders do magic. They cannot bear the touch of steel. It dampens a wielder's magic and causes physical pain for some. Some cannot even be in the same room with it, especially in the quantity that is stored in the armory. A swordwielder is a very rare thing. A swordwielder is someone who, in addition to wielding magic, cannot only bear the touch of steel, but uses it as part of their offensive and defensive arsenals. There is less than one swordwielder to every hundred wielders. We have three at the Academy, including you, out of three hundred fifty wielder students."

If Lora thought she had been overwhelmed before, that was nothing compared to how she felt now. "What does this mean for my training, Lord Everett? Am I to be sent away?" She could not look him in the eye.

"Of course not," he said with a dismissive gesture. "Being able to do both makes you a much more important asset to the kingdom than if you can only do one. You will receive instruction in both. Your road will be harder than either alone, since you'll be expected to learn twice as much—and more—in the same amount of time."

"And more?"

He nodded and held his arm out to her. "Yes. For a swordwielder, neither of your disciplines exists by itself. You won't be just wielding or just doing swordsplay. Once you master both, you'll be integrating them." He led her to a building next to the armory. "So I guess, you'll even be on an accelerated course of study, since you'll be expected to master each discipline prior to integrating them and do all of this in the same amount of time it takes a student to master one or the other." He opened the door and led her into an office. "Lord Stephan?"

The biggest man Lora had ever seen stood from his desk. He was even larger than Gregory, the village blacksmith in Haven Dale. She felt his eyes scan her slight frame and blushed at his scowl.

"Everett," he grumbled. "I do not recall being informed I was getting a new student today, if that's what this is."

Lord Everett smiled. "This is Lorana of Haven Dale, distant cousin of Lord Allistair. She came here for wielder training, but was able to handle a dagger on our little trip through the armory. So she'll be staying in your barracks with the girls and training with Dain and Louis."

Lord Stephan's eyes narrowed. "Another swordwielder then? I've never heard of three being at the Academy at the same time." He stroked his goatee thoughtfully. "Well, I suppose Master Dain will be gone in a year or two and Master Louis' small skill with magic doesn't require much teaching beyond rudimentary, but still. Unusual." He turned toward Lord Everett and sneered. "I'll have the house mistress show her to the girl's dormitory. I suppose we will meet with Lady Demetria later to put together her schedule?"

"Sounds like a fine idea," Lord Everett replied. It was obvious he was trying to keep his exasperation out of his tone. "I'll have one of the servants bring her things here from the wielder's dormitory and show her around the grounds. I'll see you later, Miss Lorana."

She tried to curtsy as he left, but nearly fell over. Lorana's cheeks reddened and she stared at the floor. She was exhausted and overwhelmed and unprepared. All she wanted was to run and hide and fall asleep somewhere.

"You will be fine, young lady," Lord Stephan told her as he held out his arm. They walked through three hallways before they stopped before a door. "These are Mistress Tabitha's rooms. If you need anything, she will help you." He knocked on the door and went inside after a voice called from within. Lora waited for him in the hallway.

CHAPTER 4

Once Lora was left alone, the tears began to fall. She was alone and far from anything familiar that she'd ever known. She felt like some kind of freak of nature once she'd found out about her unusual status. She knew that the other young people she would be studying with would find out she was a fraud and that terrified her. She wiped her nose with her hand and sniffled.

At that moment, Lord Stephan and Mistress Tabitha emerged. They exchanged glances, and Lord Stephan bowed gracefully and left. Mistress Tabitha wrapped her arm around Lora's shoulders and ushered her into her rooms. "There, there, Miss Lorana," she said softly. "'Twill be alright. You'll make friends with the others and get into the swing of things in no time." She smiled.

Lora sniffled. "I miss my family. I don't belong here," she choked out.

"Nonsense," she said as she patted Lora's arm. "Everyone has to start somewhere. You'll see where you measure up to the others soon enough. As for your family, I assume you're not speaking about your cousin. You'll see her often enough." When Lora took in a shuttering breath and began to hiccup, Mistress Tabitha laughed. "Your family, do they call you Lorana?"

She shook her head. "My father calls me Lora," she whispered, terrified that she was disobeying Lord Allistair and Lady Tiana. "My cousins told me that name is too common and to go by Lorana here. I don't like it," she confessed.

"Then you shall be known as Lora," she declared. "There are plenty of students who have nicknames. Oh, there you are Bobby. This is Miss Lorana. She prefers Lora. You'll be getting her acquainted with the Academy." She looked at her charge. "I'd have a student do it, but they're all at their afternoon lessons." She patted Lora on the cheek and shooed her out of her rooms.

Bobby, it turned out, was quite the talker. He led her into the girl's dormitory, something that made Lora feel quite uncomfortable even though he assured her multiple times that as long as it wasn't after hours, male visitors were allowed in the girls' common areas and vice versa. The sleeping areas were off limits except for circumstances such as this. The dorms were large, open rooms with little privacy

anyway, so even though Bobby was inside, there was no place to hide

and make mischief. It wasn't until the fourth year that rooms were

made private and mischief could more easily take place.

"You'll be here between Miss Catty, er, Miss Catherine and

Miss Jane," Bobby explained. "Princess Sylvane is across from you. Did

y'know that both Prince Regan and her take swordsplay? They live

here because it's too far from the castle for them to get here when

lessons start."

"Do you study swordsplay?" Lora asked, her shyness slowly

melting away.

Bobby laughed. "They don't take commoners here," he

explained. "Commoners might learn if they join the castle guard or the

army, I suppose. I work in the stables." He smiled and led her out of

the dorms.

Their next stop was the armory. They didn't speak with

Master Blaine, as he was too busy to be bothered with a stable boy and a student. An apprentice measured Lora for her chainmail and leathers, as well as her weapons. She was dismayed to learn that she was expected to be passable with everything by the time she was finished with her studies. The axes and maces were the most daunting until the apprentice informed her that hand-to-hand combat and wrestling were usually the most challenging. The thought of no weapons being harder than weapons made Lora want to run for the hills. It seemed there would be no respite for her.

Once they left the armory, Bobby took her by the practice yards. There were many groups practicing at various stations. Older students were practicing on horseback with the lance and other weapons. Others practiced with swords, axes, maces, and even flails. Still others were using longbows, cross bows, throwing knives, spears, and funny things she had no name for. A group of students around her own age appeared to be practicing throwing each other. Lora swallowed and asked Bobby if they could look at something else. He chuckled and they moved on.

Various buildings were named on Bobby's tour. All students were expected to learn theory of war, history, higher level mathematics, and literature, among other things. The wielders learned theory of magic, and once their aptitudes were tested, they further divided based on their skills. Bobby pointed at a building off on its own that was surrounded by scaffolding. It was also the only building made of stone.

"Firewielders," he explained. "Otherwise instead of just repairing the odd wall from an explosion, we'd be constantly rebuilding the whole building if it was wood. Did I hear you could call fire?" When she nodded, he whistled. "Useful skill."

"Is there an outdoor area where the wielders practice?" Lora asked, her fingers in her mouth. When she realized she'd been chewing her nails, she sighed. She hadn't even made it through the first day.

Bobby laughed and pointed at her hand. "How old are you?"

"Twelve."

"I figured you had to be young," he explained. "The older ones don't bite their nails." Lora blushed and he continued. "There isn't a designated spot. The wielders kind of practice all around. Inside, outside. Here, on ships, in other towns. Wherever they are needed and there's someone who can teach them, I guess. Well, that's mostly it. It's dinnertime for you guys now, so I'll leave you at the dining hall. You have to leave your steel stuff outside. It offends the wielders, but otherwise there are no rules other than what you'd expect. No throwing food. Wait until the headmaster speaks before serving yourself."

Lora nodded. "Thank you for showing me around. How do you know all of this?"

"I was born here. Mistress Tabitha's my mum," he told her proudly. "I've worked in nearly every area of the Academy, too. I like the horses best, so that's where I've been for the last two years. I'm almost sixteen, and I'm hoping to be taken on permanently when my birthday comes." He sighed and pointed to a low building that groups of young men and women were entering. "There. Just follow them in and sit with some girls your age. There are plenty of you, so it shouldn't be hard." He grinned and left her alone.

She swallowed and stared at the entrance. Lora couldn't muster up the courage to walk over. She wasn't the outgoing type amongst people she'd known her whole life, and she was positively petrified of interacting with strangers. Especially strange nobles.

"Are you new here?"

Lora turned and found herself looking up into a young man's smiling face. He looked a few years older than her and hand blond hair that flopped into his eyes. She nodded.

He pushed his hair out of his face only to have it flop down again. "Come on, I'll take you in. We're nearly late, and Lord Everett hates tardiness. You can sit with my sister. I'm Regan. You are?" he offered her his arm.

"Lorana," she squeaked. "Of Haven Dale. But everyone calls me Lora." She stared at his arm like it was a viper.

Prince Regan rolled his eyes. Or at least she thought he did, as they were obscured again by his hair. He grabbed her and tugged her toward the dining hall. Once they were inside, he quickly deposited her at a table next to a couple of girls and rushed off to join his friends. A blonde girl, whom she could only assume was Princess Sylvane, opened her mouth to speak, but closed it again when Lord Everett stood up from the table where he was sitting.

"Let us bow our heads and give thanks to the gods," he said quietly once everyone was seated. A tardy student rushed in and Lord Everett's eyes narrowed. "Lucas of Green Meadows," he said, his voice even. "This is your third tardy this month. In addition to helping the kitchen staff with clean-up tonight, you will also help set up the practice yard for the swordsplayers every morning for a sevenday." When Lucas nodded glumly, Lord Everett continued, "Let us give thanks." He bowed his head in prayer.

Lorana quickly bowed her head so as not to attract notice. Her eyes flitted back and forth between Lucas and Lord Everett. She was thankful she wasn't washing dishes, but she hadn't decided if she was thankful for anything else. She was too out of her element to even consider her current situation.

Lord Everett raised his head and looked around the room. He seemed satisfied. "You may eat," he said. He sat down, turned to his left, and began a discussion with the man next to him.

"New girl," the blonde said as she served herself what appeared to be a meat pie. "Who are you? What program are you in?" She spooned some potatoes on her plate. "Wielder? Swordsplayer?" The brown haired girl on her left and the girl with curly black hair on her right leaned in to hear as they piled food on their plates.

"I'm Lorana of Haven Dale," she replied as she reached for a meat pie. The lie of her name was getting easier every time she said it. "I'm called Lora though." She paused, unsure how to describe her role at the Academy. "I came here as a wielder. I, um, keep setting things on fire."

"You'll be with me then," the girl with the curly black hair said with a smile. "I'm Genea—"

"Genea is my cousin," the blonde girl interrupted. "It's too bad you won't be in swordsplay with Catty and me. I'm Sylvane."

"Oh, but I will!" Lora replied, her mouth full of meat pie. She could not believe she was talking to the princess! "They say I'm a swordwielder. I found out when I got here. The armorer handed me a dagger and I took it like it was nothing. I didn't know I wasn't supposed to be able to do that."

Sylvane dabbed her mouth with a napkin. "What hole did you crawl out of that you didn't know what a swordwielder was? Probably the same hole where it's acceptable to talk with your mouth full and spatter food all over everyone?" She rolled her eyes, cut a small piece of pie, and daintily placed it in her mouth with her fork.

Lora's cheeks burned. She hadn't bothered with her fork, which seemed to be made of some unusual material. It made sense, considering only about half of the people in the dining hall would be able to use a steel one. "I'm only distantly related to Lord Allistair," she said in a small voice. "Where I'm from, we don't..." She looked down at her plate.

"I don't see why everyone thinks country manners are so charming," Sylvane added.

Catty, the brown haired girl on the princess's left, frowned. "Leave her alone, Sylvane. She's new, and I bet she's tired."

"Fatigue doesn't excuse ignorance or ill manners," Sylvane said. She stared at Catty for a moment and shook her head. Genea sat by looking uncomfortable.

"I'm sorry if I offended you, your highness," Lora said as she stared at her plate. She didn't touch any of her food after that and was glad when a bell rang signaling the end of dinner.

Sylvane and Genea left quickly, but Catty lingered. "The princess puts on a lot of airs, but she's mostly alright. I was her prime target before now. I'm sorry you've become that." She held out her hand and shook Lora's. "I'm Catherine of Arbor Cove. My father's barony is small, unimportant, and remote. At least that's what Sylvane tells me. But then again, she's never been to my home." She winked. "Please call me Catty."

"Thank you." Lora stood up and smiled at the girl who would be her friend.

Catty smiled back. "Come on," she said. "I'm sure you've forgotten where the dorms are by now. I'll help you learn your way around. Did Bobby give you the tour?" When Lora nodded, Catty said, "Good. He's the best."

Lora followed Catty to the swordplayer's dormitory. She was glad to see her things were next to Catty's. There was a large stack of books on her bed with a folded sheet of parchment on top. She picked it up and it appeared to be her schedule.

Catty peered over Lora's shoulder and whistled. "That's a rough schedule," she said. "I take back anything I ever prayed about wanting to be a swordwielder. If that's what it takes to be one, count me out!" She stopped laughing when she saw Lora's stricken expression. "I'm sure you'll be fine. Tired, but fine. Dain and Louis can help you. Well, more Dain than Louis. Louis' wielding ability is so small that he doesn't take classes in that anymore. Dain's nice." She leaned in and whispered, "And handsome."

Lora's schedule included history, mathematics, literature, diplomacy, theory of war, weapons, horsemanship, unarmed combat, theory of wielding, and independent study wielding. "Independent study?" she wondered aloud.

"It's probably trying to figure out what your aptitudes are and then figuring out how strong you are. Then it's probably fine tuning your best skills," Catty put in with a shrug.

"What does aptitude mean?" Lora asked. Her mouth was turned down in a frown. Her previous schooling had only been a few mornings a sevenday. This schedule had her busy from sunup to sundown and sometimes after, depending on the day, six days a sevenday.

Catty gave Lora an incredulous look. "Your strengths. What you're good at." She paused. "Did you say you lived in the keep with your cousin or were you somewhere else because—"

"Let's see your things, Lora," Sylvane said as she strode over. "I'm curious to see what the latest fashions from Haven Dale are." She pushed Lora out of the way and opened her trunk. She pulled out one of her everyday dresses and began shrieking with laughter. "Ready-made!"

Lora blushed bright red. She wasn't sure why it was such a big deal. The ready-made things were far nicer than her usual clothes, but the princess's reaction told her that the garments were something to be ashamed of. She felt terrible because Lord Allistair and Lady Tiana had been so generous.

Sylvane tossed the offending dress onto Lora's bed and continued laughing as she took the remaining items out of the trunk. "Only four gowns in here? How tragic." She walked over to Lora and looked her right in the eyes. "And your hair. Such an ugly brown. It matches your eyes." She grabbed Lora's hand and held it up. "And your nails!" She laughed some more and dropped Lora's hand. "Are you sure you're related to the Haven Dale family? I can't imagine why Tiana would claim you as a relation. I sure wouldn't!" She shook her head and chuckled all the way to her bed.

Hanging her head in shame, Lora began to gently fold her things and place them back in the trunk. She got out her nightclothes and quickly put them on. Mistress Tabitha came in and extinguished the lamps, and Lora lay down to sleep. Only once it was dark and the sounds of quiet, even breathing were the only audible sounds did Lora let the tears fall.

CHAPTER 5

The day started off terribly. In literature, Mistress Flora had Lora read aloud from the book of poetry her age group had been studying. By the time she finished struggling through the poem, the entire room was laughing, with the exception of Mistress Flora, who looked stricken. Lora sat down and stared at her desk for the remainder of the hour. After class, Mistress Flora assigned her an easier book. When Lora looked up from the book of fairy tales, her teacher managed a small smile.

"Interpret them beyond the words on the page," she said. "It's as good as any place to start. I assume you've only had the basic schooling given to the commoners in your village?" When Lora nodded, Mistress Flora shook her head. "That's a shame. You will have to work harder in all of your classes than the others if you want to keep up. You can do it though. In spite of your lack of skill, you never gave up with that poem. Remember that." She patted her on the cheek and shooed her off to her next class.

Lora's next class was history. Fortunately, Mistress Diane, her teacher, did not have her read aloud. It was hard enough to follow along with the lecture. History was a neglected subject for commoners, so most of what was discussed was new to her. Commoners were usually just sent off to war without any explanation as to why their lords were sending them. They had vague knowledge as to who the king was and who was to follow him to the throne, but never they why's or how's. Lora thought it might be interesting... once she could figure out the more difficult words in the text.

Mathematics was marginally better. Lora had a decent grasp of arithmetic because she managed her father's bookkeeping. It seemed many of the nobles had as rudimentary a knowledge of sums as she did, especially Princess Sylvane. This brought Lora a perverse kind of happiness, for which she immediately felt ashamed. No matter what she did to her, Lora knew she shouldn't have any disrespect toward the princess. That was the sort of thing that brought you the sign against evil from the villagers she grew up with. Master Charles seemed a decent sort though. He was young and spoke with a lisp, but no one seemed to mind.

Theory of war was taught by Lord Cedric of Horn Peak in a huge lecture hall. He was the uncle of the current lord of Horn Peak, and evidently had a brilliant mind for strategy. He was singlehandedly responsible for keeping the Korlisseans out of Ydris and was always brainstorming ways to bring the Ydrisans on the offensive and get rid of the Shaadi threat once and for all... Whatever that meant.

Lord Cedric was charismatic, and Lora liked the fact that he did not believe in textbooks. He spoke from experience and told better stories of history than Mistress Diane did. She felt like the two classes would complement each other—at least she hoped they would. She needed all the help she could get! The worst thing about the class was the sheer amount of people in it. It was intimidating.

Master Franklin taught diplomacy. It was good thing it was just before lunch when everyone's empty stomachs kept them awake, because he was dull as unsweetened porridge. His voice droned on and on. He also made references to historical events and theory of war, but his presentation made the connections between the three very vague and uncertain. He had two texts full of required readings. It was instantly Lora's least favorite class of the day.

Her morning classes repeated daily, so she had a certain idea of what to expect each morning. It was her afternoon and evening classes that worried her. She had never done anything like any of them and just knew she'd be an even bigger failure there than she was with her book learning. She was pondering this as she wandered into the dining hall.

"Are you Lorana?" a tall boy asked her. When she nodded, he smiled. "I'm Dain. I'm the other swordwielder. I'm glad to meet you. It'll be nice to commiserate with someone else in my situation. Everyone in my age group whines about their classes, but they have no idea." He brushed his curly auburn hair back with his fingers. "It's too bad you're so young. What are you, thirteen?"

Lora knew her mouth was hanging open, but she didn't care. Dain was nice, handsome, and he was talking to her. He mustn't have heard about her morning then. "Twelve," she said shyly.

He shook his head. "Brutal," he sighed. "I was thirteen when I came. I never realized I'd been wielding. I came to be trained in swordsplay. No one could get any sword thrusts past me even though it was obvious I was not very good at it. Turns out, I was manipulating the air like a shield." He shrugged. "It's too bad, well, not really bad for me, but I'll be going off on assignment next year. I'll be out of the books and into the real world. You'll be alone. It's not so bad. Maybe they'll get another swordwielder before you leave. Louis takes theory, but his wielding ability is weak, so he doesn't specialize or practice really." He took a deep breath. "I talk a lot."

"That's alright," Lora said. "It's nice to have someone to talk to. Haven Dale is small, and I feel very out of place here." And you don't know the half of it, she finished silently.

Dain nodded. "Everyone feels out of place at first," he agreed. "Come on, you can sit with my group and get to know some more people." He led her into the dining hall toward a noisy table across the room from where Catty, Genea, and Sylvane were sitting.

"You survived your first morning, I see," a familiar face said in between bites of stew. Prince Regan smiled and actually seemed genuinely happy to see her again. She couldn't believe she hadn't made the connection as to who he was. He seemed a little more down to earth than his sister, so she hoped he wasn't too offended by any slight she might have given him.

She smiled back as she took her seat next to Dain. "Barely," she replied. "I don't read as well as most people, I'm a poor historian, and I might fall asleep in diplomacy in spite of being so hungry. Mathematics is fine, and I think Lord Cedric is just amazing. So it could've been worse."

Regan and Dain nodded, and Regan said, "Lord Cedric is the best teacher here. Even if strategy isn't their thing, everyone loves his class."

"So what do you wield?" Dain asked. "Water? Earth? Healing?"

"Let her answer, Dain!" Regan teased the older boy.

"Fire," Lora giggled. "I kept setting our house and the village on fire. My father and Lord Allistair agreed I should come. If nothing else, to learn some control so I didn't burn everything to the ground."

"Probably a good idea," Regan told her. He stuck his tongue at out at someone behind her. "Why is my sister glaring daggers at you?"

Lora looked down at her hands. "My manners are not… They're not to her liking. My upbringing was not as formal as most."

Dain rolled his eyes. "Her highness is always preoccupied with status, and she is acutely aware that no one, except Regan here, outranks her. She likes to rub it in. If she's been unkind to you, don't take it to heart. She doesn't like being out of the spotlight, so she torments anyone who's new and anyone who might take away her attention for any other reason."

"Like a swordwielder," Regan put in when Lora's gaze remained fixed on her hands. "So buck up. She's jealous. Of you." He speared a potato wedge with his fork and put the whole thing in his mouth. "Well, you'd better eat up. You'll have to change before the afternoon classes begin. Can't learn to swing a sword very well in a dress."

CHAPTER 6

There were three sets of tunics and pants on Lora's bed when she hurried there after eating. She placed two of them in her trunk and quickly donned the third set. They were all a dull brown, but she figured that was to hide dirt and sweat. And blood.

Weapons was Lora's first class of the afternoon. Lords Leonard, Nestor, and Sebastian were her instructors. She thought they seemed stern, but she figured they'd have to be since they were teaching students to defend their lives. And to kill.

Lord Leonard taught bladed weapons, including the sword, axe, spear, and knife. Lord Nestor taught blunt weapons, including the mace, morning star, flail, and quarterstaff. Lord Sebastian taught projectile weapons, including the bow, crossbow, throwing blades, and atlatl. Lora had a short one-on-one with each of them to assess her strengths and weaknesses, and then she was sent to the practice yard to learn with her age group. Lord Nestor's assistant, Master Oliver, was discussing the finer points of a quarterstaff.

Lora was vaguely familiar with the quarterstaff. It was a commoner's weapon, but Master Oliver explained that you needed to be able to use whatever was on hand to defend yourself and press on the offensive. Many infantry carried quarterstaffs and if a swordsplayer was able to disarm someone carrying one, he or she should be able to use it if needed. Being a girl, Lora hadn't been trained to use one in her village, but she knew how to hold one properly. And how to quickly duck out of the way of an inexperienced user. There was no sparring learned, as this was the first day they were using this weapon. Lord Nestor and Master Oliver drilled them on proper hand placement and stances until Lora felt like her arms were going to fall off.

Her weapons class went surprisingly fast, and before she knew it, Lora was walking to unarmed combat with the boy who had practiced next to her. He had nearly whacked her in the head several times when he lost his grip on his quarterstaff. He seemed a decent sort though. His name was Peter.

The unarmed combat instructor was called Master Karl. He was a tall lean man who appeared to be made entirely of muscle. He had sharp angular features and lanky brown hair, similar to Lora's own. His severe features made him look mean and angry, but he had a light, pleasant voice and was quick to smile and encourage.

Master Karl separated the girls and boys for the first half of the lesson. He explained to Lora that because women will never have the upper body strength of men, they need to be taught differently. Breaking a hold or throwing a punch with the same force a man would requires different techniques and if they learned both or the opposite technique right away, it would cause confusion. Other techniques were saved for more advanced lessons. Lora was paired with Catty for the first half of class and Peter for the second. She was drenched in sweat by the end.

Catty laughed at Lora and dragged her to horsemanship. Lord Ian explained that she would be learning basic riding techniques, advanced riding, jousting, and care and basic first aid for her horse. She was disappointed to be paired up with a very slow, older horse, but did not feel so badly when she realized all of her classmates had similar mounts. Lora quickly learned that like in mathematics, not all of her peers had the same experience with riding. She was pleased to be in the middle of the pack and to not draw any more attention to herself.

Lora found herself being dragged to dinner by Catty after classes were done. They sat away from Sylvane and Genea with Peter and a few others from their class. She could barely eat dinner for answering all the questions from her very curious classmates. She had some offers for tutoring in literature and history, which made her feel embarrassed and pleased at the same time.

She remembered to use her fork when she finally began to eat her meat pie. Not that it mattered to the rest of her table. Everyone was ravenous and ate how they were comfortable. A few of the boys even belched aloud.

When dinner ended, Catty dragged her back to their dormitory. "Now, we study. We're fortunate nothing got assigned today but some practice mathematics problems. Usually Mistress

Flora and Mistress Diane give essay questions. Tonight, we can catch up on Master Franklin's diplomacy readings. Everyone's always behind in that."

Lora nodded, dreading the thought of so much reading and writing. She figured she'd get more proficient at some point, but the struggle to get there was more daunting than she could have imagined. She quickly bathed and finished her mathematics, and read the first of her fairy tales. Catty told her she was jealous of that particular assignment because, "Poems are dull." Lora started on diplomacy once she had finished her fairy tale and woke up a while later with a diplomacy text on her lap. Catty shook her shoulder to tell her lights out was in a few minutes. Lora was dismayed to realize she had so much more reading to do, but Catty reassured her that she almost always fell asleep reading diplomacy. She said there was generally someone who was able to stay awake who went around waking people up in time for them to get into their nightclothes and into bed.

"That's a relief," Lora told her and she pulled her nightgown on. She did not remember getting into bed, but when morning came, she felt like she hadn't slept at all. And she hurt everywhere.

Lora had participated in strenuous activities before. She climbed trees and ran and swam, but her body was not used to the abuses it had taken the previous day. She hurt in places she had never been aware were a part of her body before. Even the tops of her toes hurt. She was glad of the day respite from swordsplay, but became really frightened when a girl at breakfast told her she would feel even worse the following day. It didn't seem possible, with how much pain she was currently in, but evidently it was.

Her morning was much the same as the day before. Mistress Flora did not call on her to read, for which she was grateful. Some other poor stuttering fool had that distinction. She recalled the names of one or two battles for Mistress Diane. Master Charles seemed pleased with her assignment, and she sat on the edge of her seat during Lord Cedric's lecture. Master Franklin's class was only interesting when he took a group of gossiping girls to task for disrupting the class and not having done the reading. Lora vowed to stay silent after that. She'd been whispering with Catty and realized that easily could have been them. She noticed that Sylvane also looked smug that it wasn't her that was caught.

Today, Catty ate lunch with Lora at the table with Dain, Regan, and Peter. "What are the wielding theory classes like, Dain?" Lora asked during a lull in the conversation.

"Hard," he said after a moment. "They really stretch your mind to its limit, and you'll be more exhausted by the end than you are after swordsplay more than half the time. It's a different kind of exhaustion. It makes it really difficult to read or do any of your other classwork unless you learn the relaxation techniques they give you. Your mind just keeps going. That can keep you awake and make you even more tired from lack of sleep."

Catty shook her head. "For the past two days I've been thankful that I only had our grueling schedule to deal with," she said. "I'm going to say it again. I'm glad I'm not you, Lora."

"Me too," Regan quietly agreed.

Peter rolled his eyes. "Every night one of your father's advisors comes here to teach you something or other. I'm pretty sure that your time at the palace on rest days is pretty well taken up with learning too," he said to Regan. "Your schedule is just as bad, if not worse."

Regan shrugged. "I guess we all have our difficulties," he said, his gaze on his cup of water. His voice was quiet. The group took that as their cue to change the subject, and they talked of the weather for the remainder of the meal.

Lora walked with Dain to her wielding theory class. She was upset to learn he wouldn't be staying with her. "I'm in a more advanced class," he explained. "Can't have you newbies learning about melding your powers before you even know what your powers are." He tousled her hair and walked down the hall.

She took a deep breath and walked into her classroom. Lora looked around and before she could take a seat in the back, she saw

Genea waving her over to her. She was relieved to know someone, even if she wasn't sure if she could call her a friend. Lora had just slid into her seat when there was an explosion in the front of the classroom.

"What did I use to do that?" came a voice from behind her. "Any ideas, Miss Lorana?" A short, bespectacled man with long grey hair was staring at her and awaiting her reply.

Lora swallowed. "Fire?"

"And?"

"Um… Air?"

"And?" When Lora gave him a blank look, he sighed. "I knew it was too much to hope for. None of you ever know anything on your first day."

Lora had a feeling that this display and his reaction were for her benefit. Why else would he draw attention to the fact that no one else knew anything either? She let go of the breath she hadn't been aware she was holding.

"Miss Genea? Anything else?"

Genea nodded. "Earth. You have to give fuel to the fire."

"Good," the grey haired man said with a nod. "What else?" When Genea shook her head, he sighed again. A red haired boy in the front raised his hand. "Yes, Louis?"

"Your essence, Lord Michael," he said without looking back.

Lord Michael smiled. "So you see, we come back to the fact that no matter what you do, your essence is a part of it. Some of you can manipulate your essence on its own, you mindspeakers, healers, and the like. You also have to remember that no element functions on its own. You might be strong in water and weak in air, but you still need the air to shape and form the water. You swordwielders need to understand this better than the others. Otherwise, you're nothing but an idiot throwing a flaming spear."

Lora's mouth fell open. This was far more complex than she had thought. And he had mentioned swordwielders! He hadn't even blinked when he said the word, unlike everyone else who changed between awed and revolted whenever the subject was brought up. It sent a chill down her spine. And the red haired boy in the front. Was he the Louis she kept hearing about? She could barely contain all of the thoughts and questions running through her mind.

"Who here can explain the concept of fire? What is fire? How does it come to be? How is it extinguished?" Lord Michael continued. When no one spoke, he tsk'ed. "Has no one done the reading?"

A plump girl a few seats to Lora's left timidly raised her hand. Lord Michael nodded at her. She wrung her hands and said, "If you please, Lord Michael, you assigned us the chapter on water."

"And why would that make a difference, Miss Violet?" Lord Michael yawned.

Violet flushed. "I..." She cleared her throat. "I don't understand what understanding fire has to do with understanding water."

Lord Michael shook his head. "That is precisely my point."

The rest of the class was a blur, and it left Lorana more confused about everything she had ever thought or thought she'd known about wielding and wielders. She stood up when it was over and shook her head, trying to break out of her daze.

"He's a little intense," Genea supplied. "He's a great teacher though. He really gets you to think. Wielding doesn't follow the normal pattern of the way things work, so he challenges us so that we look at it differently." She paused. "At least I think he is. I hope he is. Sometimes I wonder if he goes to his rooms and laughs after our classes."

Lora smiled and took her fingers out of her mouth. She hadn't even realized she'd started chewing her nails. She winced. "Will the independent study be like that?"

"Only if you get Lord Michael for it."

She found that both exciting and terrifying. Lora sighed. "I have Lord Jeremy. What's he like?"

Genea's eyes brightened. "He's young. Just barely graduated

from here. He's so handsome! You'll just love him." She placed a

hand on her chest and pretended to swoon.

CHAPTER 7

Lora hated him. Lord Jeremy's voice was nasally. His dark blond hair was long and curly. Too curly for it to be natural. She was certain the mole on his cheek was fake. He wore a tunic in a shocking shade of green she had no name for. It had more lace than even the fanciest of Lady Tiana's gowns. He paired it with hose that she swore had dogs painted on them. And he wore shiny white gloves.

She appeared to be alone in her lack of admiration for the man. The other three girls in the class gave him dreamy looks all during his lecture. The three young men looked bored.

"So Miss Lorana," he said after he introduced himself to her. "Before we do anything, we need to figure out where your strengths lie. I've heard fire. Set a few buildings in your village on fire, I'm told. As well as some curtains."

"Yes, Lord Jeremy," Lora replied as her face flushed red and her hands covered what they could of her face. She was so embarrassed to have the things she was ashamed of brought out in front of strangers. Strangers she would have to work with for the duration of her time at the Academy.

"I also read that you knocked over an antique vase with a gust of air?"

Lora hated the way he pronounced vase like vahz. She wondered if he knew how much of an ass he sounded like. "Yes."

"Nothing else?"

"No."

A look of dissatisfaction crossed Lord Jeremy's face. He walked over to Lora and placed his hand on her forehead. She felt a cold sensation and then a jolt of something so strong that she cried out and tried to rip his hand from her. He held firm and closed his eyes. By the time he was finished doing whatever it was that he doing, she was in tears again.

"Very interesting," Lord Jeremy mused. "Very interesting indeed." He steepled his fingers and tapped them together. "All five. All strong. I'm not sure what direction the essence will go. You don't seem the healer type. I think you're more of a mindspeech type or a distance talker. But I've been wrong about essence before." He walked back to the front of the room and began giving everyone their assignments for the day.

At dinner, Lora picked at her food. She had been excited to learn about wielding, but Lord Jeremy made it feel dirty and disgusting. She sighed for about the tenth time and set her fork down. She took a big drink of her water and sighed again.

"Alright," Dain told her. "Enough with the sighing, Lora. What gives?"

She met his eyes and said, "Lord Jeremy is my independent study teacher."

"So?"

"I don't like him."

Dain chuckled. "You must be the only girl at the Academy who doesn't."

"He dresses fancier than the princess."

Regan threw his head back and laughed so hard tears came to his eyes. "You can't deny she hit the nail right on the head there, Dain." He wiped his eyes and coughed to get his countenance back. "That can't be all though."

Lora spooned a huge bite of stew into her mouth and chewed noisily on a potato. She ignored Catty's wince at her manners. "He put his hand on my head. It was gross."

"That happens to everyone," Dain told her.

"Yeah, but do they make a big deal out of what they see in everyone?"

Dain shrugged. "It depends on what they see."

Lora was silent. Thoughtful.

"So tell us what he saw already!" Catty said. Her exasperation was palpable.

"All five elements. All strong," Lora said. Her voice was soft and she stared at her hands, kicking herself for the state of her nails.

The table was silent. After a moment, Dain cleared his throat. "I don't know of any but Lord Michael who can control all five. Well, maybe one or two others, but he's the only one who's strong in all of them."

"Oh," was all Lora could say.

A bell rang and everyone groaned. "Come on," Catty told Lora. "Everyone's favorite! Etiquette."

Lora had thought she'd been way behind in literature and history, hopeless in swordsplay, and confused in theory of wielding. She couldn't have been. She had never been more inept, hopeless, or confused about anything as she was about etiquette and protocol.

First came the bowing and curtsying. There was a bow and a curtsy for all ranks and occasions, and all were different. With her real status, it was easy. Curtsy so low she was nearly sitting on the floor for everyone but Regan and Sylvane. Fall on her face and grovel before them. With her new elevated status as a minor noble and swordwielder, it was more complicated.

The style and mechanics of her curtsy were off, Mistress Diane told her. One curtsied deeper to an ambassador at an official function than to a duke, but in an informal setting, the curtsy to both was only as deep as one you'd give your peers. You gave your peers a curtsy with the knees bent at a thirty degree angle and held it for one breath. Arm flourishes were out of fashion. No one gave a head nod except the royal family.

Lora felt as if her heart was going to pound out of her chest. Her hands shook, which she could not hide when she spread her skirts for her curtsies. She blinked back tears. Nothing made her stick out, nothing betrayed her origins more than this class.

Peter was her current partner. He frowned and took her hands in his. "Lora, what's wrong?"

She took a deep breath. And another. "I've never done this," she confessed. "My family... We never socialized with L—Cousin

Allistair or his guests." She got as close to the truth as she dared. "Our home was not formal. We had no occasion to cross paths with anyone important. Not until I set the thatching of my neighbor's home on fire and Cousin Allistair became involved. I never had any real schooling. I've only ever read the school primer." Lora hung her head and shook his hands away from hers. Her voice was no louder than a whisper.

"It's alright," he told her awkwardly. "Everyone's backgrounds are different. Not everyone can be in the main branch of their family. Not everyone here is landed. I'd say half live no better than the wealthy commoners in their villages."

"Yes, but at least they know how to curtsy!" she said as she wiped her nose with her hand. "Sorry," she told him as she wiped her hand on her dress.

Peter shrugged. "As you say, you'd no occasion to do it at home." He smiled at her. "Cheer up. We'll help you."

Lora shook her head. "That's all anyone's been doing since I got here. Helping me catch up." She took a couple of deep breaths and counted to ten. "How can I learn what I need to if I'm struggling to catch up? How can you learn anything if you're all trying to help me?" She squeezed her eyes shut. "I should go back home."

"And burn down your village?" Peter asked. He was sorry there was no way to ask that gently.

"I know I have to stay," she admitted. "I knew it would be hard. I just didn't know how hard."

"It will get better."

"It'd better." She managed a wan smile.

Peter chuckled and bowed. Lora shook her head. "I'm lower ranked. I curtsy first." She paused. "Right?"

"You learned something after all," he teased.

Lora looked thoughtful. "I suppose I did."

CHAPTER 8

The next day was similar to the first. Her morning was dedicated to book learning, while the afternoon was dedicated to swordsplay. Lora had assumed that swordsplay was, well, fighting with a sword. It made her head spin to think of all of the different ways of fighting and to think that she would have to be proficient in all of them, as well as be able to integrate her wielding abilities with all of them. Her new friends were the only thing that got her through.

Lora had been picked by Mistress Diane to debate the cause of the war with Korlisse with a girl she didn't know. The material had not been in the reading, which Lora had been too tired to complete anyway. It was something that was hotly debated in noble circles, knowledge that was apparently taken for granted.

"Money," Lora said the first thing that came to her mind.

The other girl rolled her eyes. "That's my angle. We already established that." She crossed her arms in front of her chest in a huff.

"But you said natural resources," Lora replied. Her voice was barely above a whisper. She wanted nothing more than to run and hide somewhere.

"Natural resources can be bought and sold. They're as good as money." The girl muttered under her breath about the stupidity of country dwellers.

Lora bit her nail down to the quick, and the tang of blood filled her mouth. She had nothing further to say. She'd barely been able to study the map in her text. She had never seen a map before and had spent much of her time looking at Ydris. Korlisse was nothing more to her than a word on paper. She had lost two uncles in that war, but she did not know why the war had taken place. She certainly didn't know how it started or about any debate over why it started.

Mistress Diane frowned. "You may sit, Lorana. You will be charged with reading extra chapters about our wars with Korlisse. Catherine, you will debate this subject with Susan."

She was relieved to sit down and embarrassed about her relief. Lora took her finger out of her mouth. The bleeding had stopped. She looked at her other fingers and all of them were in similar shape. Frowning, Lora started counting, as Tiana said she should.

That afternoon, Lora was given an atlatl and darts and told to think of the weapon as an extension of her arm as she hurled the darts toward a target. By the end of her lesson, she had started getting her darts close to the target. She considered this progress.

She was quiet at dinner in spite of her new friends' attempts to draw her out. She answered in one word, one syllable responses when she was able, and she barely touched her food. She only brightened when Peter mentioned he was going to study in the library.

"Library?"

Peter nodded. "Yes, it has a bunch of tables and chairs and stuff in it. Good places for studying when you're trying to stay awake," he told her.

"Can I come with?" she asked.

"Of course."

Lora smiled. She had a vague recollection of seeing the library with Bobby, but with everything that had happened over the last few days, she had forgotten about it. If what Peter said was right, it would be easier to stay awake there and she might actually finish her assignments. The whole table decided it would be a good idea and they agreed to meet at the entrance once they had bathed and changed. Everyone was always too hungry to bother before dinner. It made for an interesting experience, but everyone was too famished to care.

When they were dressed, Catty grabbed Lora's arm and slung hers through it. "You haven't been yourself since history," she told her friend. "Forget about the debate."

She shook her head. "I didn't know what they were talking about."

Catty winced. "So you've led a sheltered life. We just have to get you up to speed. Maybe talk about politics during meals. Something other than listening to Dain's one-sided verbal dialog. Etiquette too."

"Did Peter talk to you?" Lora asked.

"Yes, he said you felt bad for asking for help," she admitted. "Don't feel bad. You're here. You have to learn this stuff. You're a swordwielder, so there's no way you'd be allowed to do anything but serve the crown. You might as well make it a little easier on yourself."

Lora ground her teeth. Service to the crown? It made sense the way everyone was going on, but it hadn't really occurred to her. What she could do was rare and valuable, so of course the king and his advisors would want to use her however they could. "Sure," she said, resigned. It would have helped if she'd wanted to serve the crown. All she wanted was to return to her village without destroying it, so anything extra was making her even more miserable than she already was.

"Good," Catty replied, giving Lora's arm a squeeze. "There they are."

She allowed herself to be guided into the library and then into a small room set aside for group study. She placed her books on the table and asked where the history section was. Once she was pointed there, Lora went in search of books on Korlisse.

Overwhelmed by the sheer number of books all in one place, Lora quickly became lost. Was it on the second floor or in the second aisle past the librarians' work area? Cursing herself for wasting valuable time, she was not paying attention and ran into something— someone.

"I'm sorry," Lora said in dismay and the person's papers spilled all over the floor around them.

She was answered with laughter. "Don't worry about it, my dear. Just help an old man pick them up. I can sort them out later."

"Lord Cedric." Lora was mortified. Her favorite teacher!

The theory of war teacher smiled. "You're new. First sevenday here, I'd say, by the look of you. Like a startled deer, you are. You must be our new swordwielder then. What are you called?"

"Lorana of Haven Dale. Lord Allistair is my cousin," she said as she gathered up the papers. She felt as meek as a mouse.

"Are you?" His eyebrow shot up in amusement, his attention taken from their task. "Are you closely related? Do you live in the keep? I've been there a number of times, and I can't recall seeing you."

Lorana swallowed. "No, we are only distantly related. I grew up in the village."

Lord Cedric nodded thoughtfully. "I see," he said. "What were you looking for, young Lorana of Haven Dale? You have helped me. Let me help you."

"The section on history," she said with a wince. "I'm behind in my studies. I need some..." She paused, trying to think of the word

Mistress Diane had used. "Realization? Especially on the war with Korlisse."

"I'm sure you do, if you grew up in the village," Lord Cedric told her. "What specifically did you need to know?"

Lora bit her lip. "Why we've fought with them. I... I was asked to sit down during class because I could not pick a side to debate. I don't know anything about the war beyond the fact that I have uncles who died fighting in the last one."

"Have you looked at a map?" he asked. When Lora nodded hesitantly, he continued. "What do we have that they don't? You can tell just by looking at the map. That will answer one of the confounded reasons for those wars."

She raised her fingers to her mouth, but found she had no nails left to chew on. Frowning, she clasped her hands behind her back. "I've only seen the map a couple of times. Twice, actually."

"The sea," Lord Cedric supplied. "They do not have access to the sea. The mountains and our country divide them from it. They wish to have access to it for trade. They have a formidable navy though, in spite of this."

"So it is about money."

"Indirectly, yes. But there are other reasons for it too. King Gerald doesn't get along with King Shane. They both like to insult each other in... indirect ways and wait and see how long it takes the other to understand the implications. There have also been some betrayals in the past."

Lora looked thoughtful. "Personal then. Kind of like why the butcher in our quarter won't speak to the blacksmith."

Lord Cedric chuckled. "I'm sure of it. You see, you don't need *remediation*, Miss Lorana. You just need a few extra details."

"My... friends are trying to help me."

"They sound like good sorts. Who have you fallen in with?"

"Catty—Catherine, Peter, Genea, Dain, and Prince Regan."

"A fine bunch," he told her. "I have been asked to call Catherine "Catty" as well. Her mother is called Catherine, and she likes to distinguish herself from her."

She hesitated a moment. "I'm called Lora."

"It's been a pleasure, young Lora." Lord Cedric smiled. "Come find me again when you have need for remediation." He patted her on the head and walked away.

Lora stared after him a moment and then walked back to the study room. She sat down at the table and opened her book of fairy tales. She had a charcoal pencil poised over a piece of parchment when Dain interrupted her thoughts.

"Couldn't you find the history section?" he asked, gesturing to the fact she was working on something other than history. "I knew I should've gone with you. The library can be confusing if you haven't been in it before."

"I ran into Lord Cedric. He... He helped me." Lora lifted her gaze and met Dain's eyes.

Regan nodded. "He does that. Helps out, I mean. Even if it's not his class, if he knows someone is struggling, he'll talk to them. Never even know he's teaching, he makes it so simple. Did he tell you what you needed to know?"

Lora nodded. "Even though I wasted time wandering around, I still saved time because I don't have to sift through a bunch of books to find what I needed." She paused. "He's nice."

"One of the best," Genea agreed.

Mistress Diane did not call on Lora to speak in class the next day. It was Lord Cedric who did.

"Miss Lorana. Lorana of Haven Dale," Lord Cedric's voice boomed. "Tell us what most would consider justification for going to war."

A few hundred faces turned to look at her and her face burned. "Money," her voice wavered.

"Can you be more specific?"

Lora took a deep breath. "Trade?"

"Is that a question or an answer?"

"An answer." She started counting in her head.

Lord Cedric turned to the blackboard behind him. "Very good. And what else?"

She was a little shocked he would ask her exactly what they had discussed the night before. He had to know that she knew the answers. She swallowed and said, "Personal. Insults and the like."

"Indeed," he replied. Lord Cedric then smoothly transitioned into a lecture on his favorite topic, the Korlissean wars, specifically the debates on what started them.

Catty lingered behind in theory of war once the rest of the group had moved on to diplomacy. She didn't particularly care if she was late. Master Franklin wouldn't notice anyway. She waited in the short line behind the students who had unanswered questions at the end of class. When it was her turn, he smiled indulgently at her.

"That was a nice thing you did for Lora," she told him.

Lord Cedric's lips twitched. "I don't know what you mean."

"She told us she ran into you last night," Catty explained. "You notice everything. You knew she just needed a little nudge. Something to let her know that she could do this."

"Lora seems a sweet girl. Her upbringing..." Lord Cedric searched his mind for a good way to say his next sentence. "Her upbringing was different than most others here. Her family's wealth is likely infinitesimal compared to really almost anyone else's here. She isn't stupid. Her schooling probably ended a couple of years ago, if I'm correct in assuming she just went to the village schoolhouse with the common children. The lessons in those schools are only one or two mornings a sevenday and they cover basic reading and arithmetic. History is not taught. Literature is not taught. She is a... very distant relation to Lord Allistair she said, so it's very unlikely she had any exposure to other nobles in the area." He paused for a breath. "She told me who her friends were. She could not have fallen in with a better group to help her along."

Catty beamed. "I like her, for all we've known each other a few days," she replied. "Her manners are coarse and she isn't well read at all. But she's sweet and she fits in with our group. Of course we'd help her. We help each other enough!"

"Make sure you let her see that the others in the group need help too," Lord Cedric told her. "She has a harder road ahead of her than most, especially considering her being a swordwielder. That seems like a good joke the gods are playing on her." He cleared his throat. "Now get along with you. Master Franklin will notice your tardiness if you delay any longer."

CHAPTER 9

The next couple of days went by in a blur. Lora was anticipating and dreading her one-on-one swordwielding class. Well, maybe not one-on-one. Dain would be there. But she was frightened all the same. She hoped the teacher was nice and not like Lord Jeremy, whom she despised.

Dain held his arm out to her after dinner the day their class was held. "You ready for this?" he asked. "It's the best of both worlds. It'll get you excited about being here if nothing else."

Lora smiled and took his arm. She tried not to be jealous of everyone rushing past on their way to study. While she wanted to learn more about her abilities, she also lamented the two hours of lost study time when she was so far behind in her classes.

She was led to a small classroom with a half dozen desks in it. In spite of the small amount of seating, it was a large room. Lora figured this was because of its dual purpose of wielding and swordsplay. They'd need to learn theory as well as practice their skills. She quickly realized they were in the stone building, which was fortuitous, considering she was strong in firewielding.

"Master Dain, Miss Lorana," a short, burly man half grunted at them when they entered.

"This is Lord Robert," Dain told her. "Lord Michael should be along soon."

Lora blinked. "Lord Michael is a swordwielder?"

Dain frowned. "I didn't tell you? I could've sworn I did. But yes, he is."

Lord Michael entered just then and gestured for them all to sit. "The next sevenday or so will be review for Master Dain here and new to Miss Lorana. You're called Lora, am I correct? Lord Cedric said something about you liking to be called something other than your given name."

"Yes," she nodded. "I go by Lora."

The two teachers looked at each other and clapped. The room was then filled with rain, thunder, and lightning. One of the desks sprouted roots and began growing through the floor. The men clapped again and all was silent. The floors were dry. The desk was no longer rooted to the floor. They then stood and drew their swords. Michael's burst into flame and he lunged toward Robert. Robert never moved. The flaming sword struck an unseen barrier and bounced off. The two men smiled and the flames in the sword died.

"Those are the basics of what we do," Lord Robert explained. "We take the best of both worlds and use it to suit our strengths. We both prefer the sword as a weapon—"

"But like you two, we can use any," Lord Michael interrupted.

Lord Robert rolled his eyes. "Yes, yes. But you will have a favorite weapon, Lora. Dain here favors the axe. So that is what we practice with him the most."

"We use applied theory of war to understand how our presence can impact a battle, both positively and negatively," Lord

Michael continued. "Nothing you learn in your other classes is left unused here."

"Even etiquette?" Lora asked.

Lord Michael laughed. "Especially etiquette. You will see how later. Now. Lord Jeremy has apprised us of your testing. Have you practiced any of the wieldings other than air and fire?"

When she shook her head, Lord Robert hmmph'ed. "I suppose it's fine considering it was only your second class yesterday. And your swordsplay classes. I know you haven't done much there either, but do you think you might favor one weapon over another?"

"The bow," Lorana blurted out. "We haven't tried it yet here, but it was popular in my village."

Lord Robert stroked his goatee. "A never ending stream of flaming arrows that don't gutter out."

"Eruptions of earth and rock wherever your arrows strike," Lord Michael added. "Arrows able to fly swift and true through hurricane force winds." He smiled. "Are you beginning to understand?"

Lora smiled. "I think I am."

"Of course, we're a long ways from that with you," Lord Michael said. "For the next while, we'll only be talking theory. Then we'll move up to very basic combinations. You have to have very firm foundations before you can move on."

"How long will that take?" she asked.

Lord Robert laughed. "You want to answer that, Dain?"

"Well..." Dain began. He bit his lip and furrowed his brow. "I don't think you let me try anything for about three years." When Lora's eye widened in dismay, he continued, "Of course, I was slower to learn than most."

"Possibly," Lord Robert said as he rolled his eyes. "But I don't think I've ever heard of anyone begin practicum before two and a half years of theory."

"Then I will be the first." Lora hoped she sounded more bold and confident than she felt.

The three men laughed. "I love to be proven wrong," Robert said with a grin. "Now, we will use Dain as an example for most things. It's good for him to reinforce what he has already learned practically. Hopefully it will wake up things he has forgotten in his fervor to perfect his axe skills. And it will be nice to focus on some of his weaker wielding skills."

"I knew having another swordwielder here was too good to be true," Dain lamented.

"You forget Louis, Dain," Lord Michael admonished. "He may only be able to make small shields of air for very short periods of time, but he is still a member of our small group. I'm hoping to get him to push himself so he might try some illusion with his gift." He turned to Lora. "He attends wielder theory classes and drops in here from time to time. He would prefer not to, but he is what he is, and it can't be ignored."

Lora let those words sink in. She clung to them and committed them to memory. If anything would get her through this, it would be that. She could not ignore what she was, common or swordwielder, so she would have to face how those things affected her. She needed to learn to use her talents. She could not blame her shortcomings on her upbringing and social status. She would have to find a way to embrace it.

CHAPTER 10

The autumn flew past. Lora's days began to blend together, and she developed a routine. Her literature was still dismal. She could not yet read anything beyond her book of fairy tales, but was able to read it cover to cover without stumbling. Her interpretations of the text were still rudimentary, but she felt good about her progress.

In mathematics, she was above average. Master Charles complimented her on her strong fundamentals. Lora was sad that she could not give credit to her account keeping for her father, but she took any praise and treasured it close. Mathematics became a kind of morning sanctuary for her.

She struggled in history and diplomacy and would have been failing both had she not continued to run into Lord Cedric on a regular basis. After the fifth or sixth time, she asked him to tutor her outright. Lora was a little mortified at her presumption, but Lord Cedric just laughed and told her he had wondered when she would get up the gumption to ask.

Lora knew her friends were helping her wherever they could, but nowhere was it more evident than with etiquette. When on the first day back after her first restday, Dain announced that his mother had set down an ultimatum for him. His table manners had become so atrocious that she was having staff spy on him, and she would have them report to her if he was not adhering to the rules. She had threatened his pocket money, so he must comply, he said. The others took his lead, which made Lora roll her eyes, but they soon set a very fine and proper table.

In addition to table manners, other aspects of proper behavior were reinforced. None of the girls in their group went anywhere without being on the arm of one of the boys. Proper bows and curtsies were required and enforced, as were proper titles. Lora was mortified to be bowed and curtsied to and called "miss" by her friends. She had no right to even that humble title, and no noble ever bent knee to a commoner. She hated lying to her friends, especially when they went to such lengths to help her. All she could hope for was to get the hang of everything soon so they could go back to eating and acting as they had in the beginning.

Her nails still remained short and jagged, the ends of her hair in tatters.

As the days grew colder, Lora found herself anticipating a visit home over the midwinter break. She hadn't seen or spoken to Lady Tiana since she started at the Academy, so she was unable to ask her when she would be able to go home. She missed her father and brother more than anything and longed to tell them everything she was learning and about all of her new friends. Lora knew they would get a kick out her knowing the prince and princess and being bowed and curtsied to by a bunch of nobles. She would have written to them, but Lord Allistair had forbidden their correspondence, even within an envelope to him. He did not want to chance questions being asked about why she was sending and receiving correspondence from a commoner named Fletcher. She had to content herself with the knowledge that they knew she was learning a lot and being well cared for and the hope that Lord Allistair would inform her if anything untoward happened to them.

The restday before midwinter, Lora found herself in the library. She always tried to avoid it on restdays, but if there were any essays due, she needed the extra time to read and write so they could be finished on time. Even though she had made many strides, she was still embarrassed about her shortcomings. She was so focused on diplomacy that she did not notice that someone had sat next to her until she felt her arm being pinched.

"Ow!" she started.

Regan chuckled, his blond hair flopping down over his eyes. "You shouldn't be in here on a restday. It's indecent. If you must practice something, do something you like. Like shooting arrows. Or something that gets you outside, like hurling a Morningstar around. Or even riding."

Lora shook her head. "Essay," she said waving her parchment at him. "You know I need the extra time on this."

"Well, you can't blame me for trying," he told her.

"What are you doing here on a restday, Prince Regan?" she asked as she put her charcoal pencil down. "Aren't you and your royal sister usually at the palace learning about... royal things?" She tried to throw the "prince" in there whenever she remembered. It was hard because he always acted so informal with everyone.

He closed his eyes and sighed. "For once, I'd rather be there. Our midwinter ball is coming up. I have never been. I'm fifteen now, so I'm expected to start making appearances. I'm here to practice dancing." When Lora snorted and laughed, he scowled. "Just you wait. I'll make sure you have to come when you're old enough." He laced his fingers behind his head. "Speaking of which, I thought I heard you tell Catty that your birthday is coming up just before midwinter's day? Are you going home to celebrate?"

She frowned. "No. It's ten days journey there and back. Almost three sevendays just in travel. I could only be there for a sevenday, so L—Cousin Allistair said no." She grimaced. "I miss my family. I am hopeful for the summer holidays. We shall see."

"You're turning thirteen, right?" he asked. When she nodded, he continued, "We should throw you a little party."

"Please don't!" Lora was shushed by an ancient librarian, and she winced. "Please don't," she said, lowering her voice back to an acceptable level. "I can't contribute to anyone else's, so it's not right for me to have one. Same goes with midwinter gifts. I'll have none of that. I get no pocket money until the Academy says I can go out into Glimmen on restdays."

Regan yanked on her skirts. "You should get some gifts," he teased. "You've grown since you got here. Your ankles are peeking out under your skirt there." He turned his nose up. "It's indecent." When he looked back at her, he winked.

Lora looked down at how her short her skirts had gotten. "I'll have to write to Cousin Tiana," she lamented. "She said she would take care of that."

He patted her on the shoulder. "At this rate, you'll end up taller than me," he teased. It was a good jest, for she was so short it

was unlikely she'd be taller than any girls of their acquaintance.
"Anyway," Regan said, changing the subject, "Can you practice these silly dances with me? Sylvane refuses to."

She shook her head. "As much as I need the practice, diplomacy calls. Maybe Catty? Last I saw her, she was headed for the stables. She may be riding or attempting to curry her horse."

"Suit yourself," he told her. Regan stood up, bowed his head, and left.

Lora bit her lip. Like Regan would rather be at the palace than dancing, she would rather be dancing than writing her essay. She picked up her pencil and then quickly set it back down. She reached into her pocket and drew out a very wrinkled, very tear-stained sheet of parchment. She flattened it out and read it again.

Cousin,

Lorana, I am pleased to hear from your teachers that you are performing adequately at the Academy. Your father and brother are well and send their regards. The keep and village of Haven Dale carry on. As to your question about visiting over your winter holidays, I'm afraid I cannot justify the expense. I will not have the wrong people notice that you are visiting with commoners. I appreciate that you have kept your word and not written to your family, but it is not worth the risk. A slip up or chance encounter could ruin all you are working toward. Because of this, you will remain in Glimmen for the summer holidays as well. Be well.

    Cousin Allistair

She wiped away the tears that sprang to her eyes every time she read the letter, and she placed it back in her pocket. She understood Lord Allistair's reasons, but she hated them all the same. Picking up her pencil, she wiped her nose on her sleeve. It was very unladylike, but Lora did not care. Diplomacy awaited.

CHAPTER 11

Her friends were respectful, and there was no birthday party. Lora did receive one gift from Catty. Catty had been upset to learn that Lora's ears were not pierced and she could not wear the ear bobs, so Jane and she held her down one night before lights out and pierced them with a red-hot darning needle. Sylvane tried to hide the fact that she was watching, but Lora saw her roll her eyes once she was allowed to sit back up and soothe the sting of her ears with some ice donated by an air and waterwielder they were all friends with. Lora was grateful for the gift, but wasn't ready to forgive her friends any time soon.

Shortly after her birthday, Lady Tiana paid her a visit. It was still winter holidays, so Lora was able to see her in the middle of the day even though it was not a restday. Her husband, Larence of Rock Harbor was visiting with friends in the city and did not accompany her. She sipped her tea and watched Lora over the rim of her cup for several minutes before speaking.

"Why did you not write that your clothes were getting too small?" she asked after a moment. "I would have seen to them. It's easy to have things sent over for you."

Lora removed a finger from her mouth and sighed. "I did," she replied. "It must have arrived after you left."

Tiana frowned. "I suppose I can take you to the tailors today," she said. She took another sip of tea and placed her cup on the table beside her. She stood up and beckoned Lora over to her. "Let's not waste time. We can talk on the way there."

It was her first time in the city. In spite of having been in Glimmen for nearly six months, Lora had never been beyond the walls of the Academy. She tried very hard not to gawk and gape at everything around her, but she could not help it.

"Stop staring, cousin," Tiana scolded. "As improper as it would be, I'm not above blindfolding you. There is a reputable tailor right around the corner. This little piece of the city is really not that exciting, so please just... walk. And get your fingers out of your mouth!

The state of your nails, Cousin Lorana. I wish I could blame them on your training, but anyone can see that you've bitten them. Have you had your courses yet?'

Lora was taken aback by the question. "No."

"Hmmm. I'm trying to decide whether it's worthwhile to get you some things for that now. It's difficult to predict, but I should say it will be soon, given that you've grown so much. Must I remind you to stay away from young men?" Tiana stared hard at her young charge.

"No, Cousin Tiana," she replied. "And I would be grateful for anything you think is necessary." Lora cold not hide her embarrassment at this topic.

Tiana sighed. "If only it weren't," she said. "Ah, here we are. Hurry along."

Mistress Bethany's tailor shop was nothing like the one in Haven Dale. It took up the entire bottom floor of the building it was in. Half of it was taken up by bolts and bolts of any kind of fabric in any color you could think of. The other half had ready-made pieces.

Lora ran her fingers over a soft rose-colored fabric and wished that Tiana would have a dress made for her rather than purchase something off the rack.

Evidently, Mistress Bethany was used to Tiana's custom for she greeted her like they were old friends. The tailor frowned when she took in Lora's appearance, but shrugged and led her to a pedestal for measurements just the same. Tiana gave her some information about Lora's age and her status as a student at the Academy. Lora tried not to wince as Tiana described her as a poor and distant relation.

"Are your nightgowns and underthings this small on you as well, Miss Lorana?" she asked as she measured. Her assistant's fingers flew as she wrote down the numbers.

"Yes," Lora admitted.

"Well, I've pieces here that will fit her for her unmentionables," Bethany told her. "But I've nothing in children's wear that will fit her. She's only thirteen. The adult dresses are inappropriate, and they would be too long. She is in between sizes in my ready-made children's apparel. I will have to have something made for her."

Lora held her breath and dared not look at Lady Tiana. The only custom made items she had ever owned were the ones her own clumsy fingers had made for her. Clothes that had been burned or given away before she left Haven Dale for Glimmen. She started to raise her finger to her mouth, but quickly brought them down and clasped them in front of her so she would not be tempted to bite her nails.

"If that's what we have to do, then that's what we have to do," Tiana told her. "Can you give me the same price as your ready-made pieces?"

Bethany nodded. "I have some inferior fabric I could use."

"And the simplest styles possible, please," Tiana told her. "The evening piece can be a little bit nicer. You and I can haggle over the sum once it's made. I'll be in Glimmen for another two sevendays.

You can have these all done by then? Four day dresses and a dinner gown?"

"I can have them done in a sevenday," the tailor replied.

Lora tried not to pay attention when Lady Tiana and Mistress Bethany started looking through fabrics and talking about styles. She knew she should be grateful to get anything at all, but she wished for something pretty. She did not want a custom made dress made out of an old burlap sack or whatever inferior fabric might be. Princess Sylvane and her friends already teased her enough. She did not want to give them any more excuses.

Exactly one sevenday later, Lady Tiana arrived to take her back to the tailors. Lora still gawked at her surroundings, but she felt that she was getting her bearings and might actually be able to find her own way to the shop. It wasn't as if she'd ever have the coin to buy anything there, but the freedom of being outside the Academy for any reason was exciting.

When they reached the shop, Mistress Bethany again greeted Lady Tiana as if they were old friends. She quickly had Lora step behind a screen and undress down to her underthings. The first dress she tried on was a hideous olive green. The material was scratchy, and she made a mental note not to scratch her neck or wrists until Lady Tiana left for the evening. When Tiana pronounced the fit adequate, she was told to try on the next garment. The dress was a goldenrod yellow in the same itchy fabric in the same exact style. Lora took a deep breath and strode out to where the women awaited her. Tiana nodded and waved her back behind the curtain. The third dress was nearly the same ugly mousy brown as her hair. It too was in the same fabric in the same style. When she emerged from behind the curtain, Tiana frowned, but then shrugged and waved her back. The last dress was an unfortunate orange color, again in the same fabric and same style. She caught Mistress Bethany's eye when she came out and the tailor had the decency to look a little embarrassed.

"Here is the dinner dress," Bethany said. "I took a few liberties here. No extra cost to you. The day dresses, well… I felt she should have something to feel pretty in."

Lora went behind the curtain and undressed. She passed back the orange nightmare, and did not look at what she received. Only when she noticed that the cloth was soft did she dare look at it. Her breath caught when she saw that it was the same rose-colored fabric she had admired when she had first come in. There were tiny roses embroidered along the neck and cuffs of the sleeves. The sash was wide and made of a shiny ribbon of the same color. Tears came to Lora's eyes and she blinked them back as she put the dress on. She took a deep breath and stepped out from behind the screen.

Lady Tiana's eyes softened. "That is quite nice," she said. "I'll pay what it is worth. It's a good color on her. I will take some hair ribbons to match, as well."

Mistress Bethany nodded. She made eye contact with Lora as she called to her assistant to fetch some ribbons, and she winked. Lora smiled back, and quickly hurried behind the curtain. Her happiness was only dampened a little bit when the orange nightmare was passed to her to wear back to the Academy.

The rest of the midwinter holidays were uneventful, as no one was around to make fun of Lora's new dresses. As soon as Sylvane arrived back from her stay at the palace, she nearly fell on the floor with laughter. "And I thought ready-made was bad!" she gasped between guffaws.

Lora stared at Sylvane with her arms crossed in front of her chest. "They may be ugly, your highness," she told her. "But they are what I have to wear. Many others are not as fortunate as I am. I have five brand new dresses made to fit me. Sure, the colors and cloth from four of them are ugly, but I don't care." She stared at the other girl until her shrieks of laughter quieted down and her smile became a scowl.

When Sylvane stomped out of the dorms, Catty put her arm around Lora. "Well done, my friend. Not even Regan can shut her up when she gets going." She pulled away after a moment. "That really does itch. How can you stand it? Is your skin made of steel?"

"My practice tunic is underneath or I wouldn't be able to stand still," she replied with a shrug. "I've got scratches everywhere from before I thought of wearing it."

Regan strolled into the dorms as he whistled a cheery tune. He stopped and blinked. "I see now what my sister was stewing about," he said as he walked over to where the girls stood and pushed his hair out of his eyes. "That is the exact same shade as your hair. I don't think you could've planned that better. You're like a... walnut."

"That's a weird thing to say, Regan," Catty said, punching him in the arm. "No woman wants to be called or likened to a walnut."

He shrugged and Lora laughed. "Well a walnut is better than the dirty grey egg yolk, the pea soup catastrophe, or the orange nightmare." She pulled each one out and set them on her bed.

Catty shook her head. "Did you commit some ghastly wrongdoing to your cousin Tiana?" She peered into Lora's trunk as if it held a treasure trove of oddities. Her eyebrows rose and she pulled out the fifth dress. "This is lovely, Lora."

Lora blushed and grabbed the dress from her friend. "I love it, but I doubt I'll ever wear it. I never leave the Academy. I guess I have to have it though—just in case. It seems a waste of money." She folded it and placed it back in her trunk followed by the three others.

"I had a thought," Regan said. He had one arm supporting the other and was tapping his chin with his free hand. "What if we start dressing the part during etiquette? All we do is practice for those events."

"I like it," Catty said. "I'm sure Dain and Peter and Genea would do it. What say you, Lora?"

"I like it, too," Lora said.

CHAPTER 12

"I'm sorry you have to stay here for the summer, Lora," Genea was saying. "I'll be around. Perhaps I can convince my father to let you stay with us for a bit. We might be going to the coast around midsummer's day. It would be fun if you could join us." She smiled and pushed a lock of black curls out of her face.

Lora shrugged. "I'm years behind where the rest of you are in my studies," she said. "I'll be better off here reading literature, practicing the sword, or curtsying to Mistress Diane until my knees snap off. Plus Cousin Allistair said he couldn't justify the expense when I asked if I could visit Catty. I can't imagine he'd change his mind for you."

Genea frowned. "Maybe if my father wrote to him…"

"You can ask if you like," Lora said. "I just think you'd be wasting your time. I get the impression that my father feels badly that he can't pay these experiences for me himself, and so even if Cousin Allistair wanted to, I don't think he'd go against my father."

Catty made a face. "Well, Dain might be staying even if I'm not. And Regan will be around."

"At the palace, not here," she said, her face glum. "Dain said he'd only be here for about a sevenday longer than everyone else. He offered to smuggle me to Mount Rathbone, but that would be too weird. Peter, well, he's Peter. He waved goodbye to me when he left yesterday." Lora sighed. "Regan might make it over here to the Academy a few times, which I suppose is better than being totally alone with the other students that are stuck here."

"How many others are staying?" Genea asked.

"Less than ten."

"Oh."

"You'll be sparring with our teachers!" Catty was dismayed. "I'm so sorry! You'll probably be broken to bits when we all get back."

Lora rolled her eyes. "Thanks for the vote of confidence. Anyway, I have to look at it as an opportunity to improve my fundamentals and technique. Or so Cousin Allistair said in his letter."

Catty and Genea hugged their friend. "Promise you'll write!" they said in unison.

Lora did, in fact, write to them. At least once a sevenday. And they wrote her in return. The boys were not such faithful correspondents, but no one expected them to be.

She practiced her fighting skills every morning when it was still cool out. She found that she was learning to appreciate the sword. Lord Leonard tried to get her to use a rapier, but Lora found she liked something with a little more substance. She also liked throwing knives with Lord Sebastian. There was something very satisfying about how a knife sounded when it hit a wooden target. Thunk! She felt a little badly that she was ignoring Lord Nestor, but she just didn't have the size or strength to swing around a mace or a flail. She thought perhaps when they started fighting on horseback.

She practiced wielding every afternoon. She was now able to call on all five elements with some effort. She couldn't do much with any of them except fire and sometimes air. Lords Michael, Robert, and Jeremy rarely agreed on anything, but they all agreed that she should spend her summer concentrating on water, earth, and her own essence. That way they would know where she was truly strong or weak, not just a guess from Lord Jeremy's assessment. They told her this was particularly true for her essence. She would not know exactly what she could do until she had practiced what they called opening up her center. It sounded like a lot of rubbish, but Lora spent a lot of time doing that too.

In the evenings, Lora read. She had long since finished her book of fairy tales. She had moved onto and finished a book of fables by the end of the school year. Now she was free to read what she pleased. She attempted a novel, but gave up after the first chapter. Genea eventually loaned her one of her own books, which was far more to her liking. She also read whatever she could on history and diplomacy. She sat with Mistress Diana and Mistress Flora at meals to practice her etiquette, and they made her follow the same rules her group had established after the winter holidays. Lora hated it, but it kept her in practice.

Genea was true to her word and saw Lora often before she left for Azure Shores. They both missed all of their other friends terribly and compared letters from each of them. They laughed for hours when they found that Dain had simply copied his letters and sent them to each girl. A quick request to Catty in their next letters to her confirmed that she indeed was receiving the same letters, too. As retaliation, they decided to just send him one letter with all three of them signing it. To continue the good fun, Dain sent three different replies. The three replies made up only one note with each girl only getting every third word. They had to combine their letters in order to decipher the whole thing. They had barely gotten Catty's letter when Genea had to leave.

Lora was quite lonely after that. Her only companions were about ten students who stayed through every holiday, and most of them kept to themselves. She knew Susan of Round Lake a little bit and had seen Lucas of Green Meadows in passing, but she was not friendly with either. She saw plenty of Bobby, who was beginning an official apprenticeship in the stables. He was eager to help her saddle and care for her horse, even though it was part of her duties as an Academy student.

One day after Lora had finished riding, she asked, "How do all of the other students not forget anything if they all go home for the summer?"

Bobby was currying the horse in the next stall over. He paused, stood up, and looked at her. "Why, they practice their swordsplay with the men-at-arms in their family keeps. Or they practice wielding with someone in their keep or village. They have libraries in their keeps, too." He paused. "Don't you?"

Lora flushed. "I did not live in the keep," she spat out. "I lived in a house in the village. I don't think Cousin Allistair would like me bothering his soldiers if I were able to go home. He says it's easier to keep me here—and sending me home is not worth the expense. I'm actually probably better off staying here. I'm behind enough as it is. He sponsors me here, so I have to do as he says."

"He sounds like a very honorable man," Bobby said. She did not have anything to say after that, so she sat watching him until he shooed her away.

The summer holidays were over soon after that. Genea returned first, quickly followed by Peter. Catty and Dain arrived on the same day. Regan made an appearance after that. Lora realized that even though they had both been in Glimmen all summer, they had not seen each other at all. His royal duties would always take precedence over socializing with friends. The group reunited in the dining hall. They all had exciting stories to share except for Lora, who just listened politely.

Regan had spent the summer training with the palace guard and helping his father make important decisions for Ydris. "Perhaps we'll discuss your contributions to society in our diplomacy class," Catty teased.

"Cruel," Regan replied with a sigh. He put his hands behind his neck and his straight blond hair flopped into his eyes. "So cruel to mock my moment in the sun. But seriously though, when I turned sixteen he made this big fuss about me starting to learn by doing. It's scary, making decisions that affect everyone's lives." He paused. "Well, maybe not any *people's* lives, but the lives of some very grateful sheep."

No one wanted to know exactly what that meant.

Genea had discovered a talent for healing. While at Azure Shores, she said she had an epiphany and was able to call on her essence to heal. In order to stay well rounded, she worked with some of the traditional healers and started learning some herb lore. "I'm not sure what my strength and skill in it will be, but it's always good to be prepared for what you might not be able to help with just wielding," she said. She was always very shy about her accomplishments, and Lora thought she ought to be less so. Genea was very sweet and deserved all the credit she could receive.

"Arbor Cove is unchanged," Catty declared as she flung her long, dark brown braid behind her shoulder. "And so am I." She went on to describe how her older brother was now taking on much of her father's responsibilities since his bout of apoplexy, but she was confident he would recover enough to take them back. "My brother, George, does not need anything else to inflate his ego. This summer, he was insufferable."

Laughing at Catty's description of his friend, Dain added, "That sounds like George alright." He cleared his throat. "Father thought he'd found a nice girl for Phillip, but he found out her family's political leanings didn't align with ours." When the rest of them looked confused, he rolled his eyes. "Shaadi sympathizers. I guess her grandmother was from Shaad, so they tend to turn a blind eye. A little more than turning a blind eye, as a matter of fact." He shrugged. "Phillip's not really the marrying kind anyway. He likes his single life." He nudged Regan in the rubs and chuckled.

Peter groaned. "Much like here, nothing happened at Lone Pine," he said with a nod at Lora. "One of the cranks in one of our smaller saw mills broke." He shrugged. "Does reading a lot count? Or practicing? I tried, but I don't think I can best Lora at archery yet."

A loud and unbecoming sniff was heard. Their heads turned toward it. Princess Sylvane tossed her blonde hair behind her shoulder. "I don't know why they bother teaching us these common weapons. The quarterstaff. The longbow. So unrefined." She sniffed again, beckoned to Genea who blushed and went to her friend, and the pair of them left.

There was an awkward pause, and then the boys took off to discuss Dain's upcoming assignment, which left Catty and Lora alone. "Still wearing the walnut, I see," Catty teased as they began the walk to their dormitory.

Lora held up her arm to show off her threadbare elbows. "I haven't grown any more, but these dresses are ready to retire. Cousin Tiana wrote that she would be here before classes started, but... As you see, she has not arrived."

"Has the orange nightmare been retired?"

"Yes," she admitted. "When I noticed them getting threadbare in spots, I wore that one the most so I'd be rid of it quicker. More quickly, I mean. The graying egg yolk is my best. It's almost as bad as the orange though."

"How is the rose?"

"I haven't worn it all summer," Lora admitted. "It felt strange without you all, and when I noticed my everyday dresses starting to wear, I was glad I hadn't, even though I'm sure I'll hear about it from Regan and Dain. I guess it's fortunate I haven't grown."

"You haven't grown?" Lady Tiana echoed as she strode into the dormitory. "Hmmm. I guess you haven't. Let me look at you." She reached for Lora's hands and frowned. "Will you never stop, cousin?" When she sighed, Catty curtsied and half ran out of the room. "Well, let us to Mistress Bethany's. You can't go around in that. I suppose the others are much the same? What about your dinner dress?"

Lora tried hard not to hope that her new dresses would be nicer than her old. "That dress is fine. I didn't wear it this summer at all. The others are like this one. Worn out."

Lady Tiana clicked her tongue. "Well, I suppose you are still a child," she said as she shook her head. "Ah, here we are."

Lora broke away from Tiana as soon as they entered the tailor's. She browsed through the more sensible fabrics on this visit. She hoped that there were either some ready-made things or that her "cousin" would be a little more generous in her choices of fabric.

In the end, two ready-made pieces were purchased, and two custom made dresses were ordered. The ready-made pieces were serviceable enough. Tan and dark blue. Plain. Not an orange nightmare in sight. It was already a winning situation, as far as Lora was concerned. She was presently surprised when a sevenday later, a wine colored dress and a dark brown dress were sent to her. Neither one itched.

She grinned at Mistress Bethany who winked. Lora hoped beyond hope that she was a kindred spirit who at the very least felt sorry for her while at the same time hoping to sell a more expensive garment. "Thank you, Cousin Tiana," she said. Her guardian was staying in town for several weeks and so was able to return to the tailor's with Lora when the dresses were finished.

Tiana nodded. "Just continue to improve in your studies, and you will be fine," she said. "Oh, did my brother write to you this summer? He has finally chosen a wife. Some Frances of Windy Heath. Even smaller than Haven Dale, I hear." She chuckled and shook her head. "Either she's uncommonly beautiful or her father is richer than he appears."

Lora nodded and followed Lady Tiana back toward the Academy. "When the time comes, Lora," she said, an awkwardness to her words, "because of your studies, you should marry well. Even though your birth is low, your accomplishments here will be enough for many families to want to associate themselves with you. So, excel in all things."

She did not know what to say, so she was silent until Lady Tiana left. Lora hoped she would be able to go back to her village and live her life once she was done training. She was beginning to feel like that wasn't going to be possible. She found Catty and explained, "She thinks I'll be able to marry better than I normally would. Do you think so?"

"You're not even fourteen," Catty replied. "You have lots of time to think about what kind of match you'd like your father—or cousin—to make for you."

"Girls in my situation marry much younger than you're used to," Lora told her. "At sixteen, even fifteen sometimes."

Catty's eyes grew wide. "That's as young as commoners marry," she pointed out. "Surely that wouldn't be in store for you. Especially considering training isn't finished here at the Academy until, well, nineteen here and twenty one or twenty two out on assignment."

Lora frowned. "That seems ancient."

"I suppose it's not," Catty said with a sigh, "or else girls wouldn't be allowed to train so long. Our fathers would be busy trying to marry us off. Maybe we wouldn't even be allowed to train anymore at all if we were supposed to marry so young. I mean, I guess girls who don't train here marry a little younger. But not at fifteen. Ugh! That would be in a year for me!"

They vowed never to speak on this topic again. It was too embarrassing for both of them. Lora could not share her situation with Catty, and Catty would not share her situation and aspirations with Lora. They both secretly thought that the other would be ready to continue the discussion in another couple of years.

CHAPTER 13

Lora was upset that even after an entire summer of practice, she was still not reading what the others in her literature class were reading. She knew that they all, including Catty, thought that she was stupid. Catty was just too polite to say so to her friend. Mathematics, as ever, was a sanctuary. They were delving into areas Lora had never even known existed, but the concepts were not too difficult for her. It made her happy that others struggled. Not because she was trying to be mean, but because it meant that she was good at something and that her background had not kept her from everything.

Her biggest delight was history class. Her reading had improved sufficiently enough, and she had spent enough meals listening in on the teachers' discussions to nearly be on the same level as her peers. Lora suddenly found the once intimidating subject to be exceedingly interesting and made her rethink her opinions on things she had taken for granted growing up.

She wondered if anything could make diplomacy tolerable. Lora's only positive thing to say about it was that because her reading had improved, it might cut down the time she spent on that class enough that she could work on others. Lord Cedric, who had been absent all summer at his estate in Horn Peak, quickly found her in the library, and they resumed their old study sessions. He seemed pleased with her progress and started to give her more complex topics to think about and discuss.

Etiquette had gotten better throughout the preceding year; however, new topics were being brought up. Dance was going to be a focus, which most of the students groaned at. A few of the girls squealed in the delight, but once they realized they wouldn't be dancing waltzes with young men they admired, they sobered up. Master Franklin came to help teach the nuances and subtleties involved in traditional dances of other countries where duty and obligation might take Academy graduates.

"Learning these dances properly," he droned on in his nasally voice, "will show your respect toward the country you are visiting. It shows a respect for their culture. Think if a contingent from... Erasteen came and would only dance to their own music. We would think them terribly impolite and it a great slight upon us. So learning these is of utmost importance. We will start with the gentle dances of our southern neighbor, Anouria. Next sevenday, we will move on to their fire dances."

Peter and Lora exchanged glances. They were usually partnered up in etiquette. Neither of them minded, as they got along really well, and where one struggled, the other was usually a help.

"I hate dancing," Lora groaned as she stepped on Peter's foot. Again. She had, in fact, forgotten how many times she had done it. "Give me a reel. That I can do. I'm not meant for all this hopping and arm waving. I'm not coordinated enough."

"It's no different than weapons," Peter said after a moment. "Except this way, you know what your opponent, or partner rather, is going to do. You move around each other and anticipate." He shrugged.

She frowned. "I never thought of it like that. Maybe I'll stop trying to lead then?" She grinned at him.

Peter chuckled. "One can hope."

The following sevenday, Dain got his assignment. When Academy students turned nineteen, they were assessed by the staff and then assigned to a person or place depending on their abilities and the needs of various nobles at the time. Being a swordwielder, Dain was in high demand. His strengths in wielding were in water, air, and distance hearing, and he was good with an axe. He was to be sent to James Lake, where skirmishes with the Korlisseans had increased. He would be relaying messages back to Glimmen and using the lake as a weapon in his arsenal if it became necessary.

"I thought we were at peace with the Korlisseans?" Lora asked. "Lord Cedric arranged all of those treaties..." Their group was walking toward dinner after a long afternoon of swordsplay.

Dain scratched his head and stopped just before the entrance. "We are at peace, but border territories are always tricky. They're easy to rile up. Too much bad blood, I guess. I'm just glad I'm not doing any negotiations or anything like that. Not one of my strengths. I do some pretty good negotiating with my axe, but that doesn't help in the long run. Have to live together, and the axe, well, only one person lives in the end during that kind of scenario. I'm not invincible, so I'd hope it were me. You just never know. So, negotiations. I'm there for backup."

Catty chuckled. "I'm going to miss you, Dain. No one talks as much or as fast as you do." Dain flushed and she laughed harder. "It's not a bad thing. It's you." She shrugged.

"My father was glad to have you as a resource," Regan said. "He always says that he wishes he could use his swordwielders in more peaceful situations, but he says it seems like you exist only to be weapons." He scuffed his toe on the ground. "I'll think of something different for you when I am king." He sighed and offered his arm to Catty.

Dain winked at Lora before he took Genea's arm. Lora scowled. She did not like being winked at. "Why does he do that?" she asked as she linked arms with Peter. "He knows I hate it. I've asked him to stop I don't know how many times."

"He's just teasing," Peter replied as he led her to her seat. "He probably thinks your frown is funny. Or something."

That meal was the last they saw of Dain that year. Lora found that she missed the winking. She started drawing eyes in her letters to him. She was no artist, but it was obvious what they were. She let Dain ask what the eyes were four times before she told him, and she kept drawing them when he started telling her to stop. She liked that they had a joke together.

The winter holidays were fairly monotonous. Lora turned fourteen with no fanfare. All of her friends were in their homes far away, and Regan was busy in the palace as always. Genea had gone to the country to visit her mother's family. The other students who stayed during the holidays did not speak to her. The cold and sleet kept her inside and out of the practice yards. In her desperation to move around, she started to practice her dances.

If Master Franklin found it odd that she danced alone in the etiquette room while he marked the floor for some unknown purpose, he did not say so. He only complained when she danced too close to where he was working. He did not comment on her progress.

Toward the end of the holiday, Master Franklin relented after Lora's incessant pestering and taught her a new dance. She was practicing in the etiquette room when she heard laughter coming from the doorway. Her steps faltered and she blushed.

"Bravo, Miss Lorana," Regan announced as he crossed the room. He was enthusiastically clapping until Lora punched him in the arm. "Ow!" he cried.

Lora crossed her arms in front of her chest. "You can't be surprised that I did that. I don't care if I just assaulted a royal person. That was very rude, your highness."

Regan grinned. "I know I can always count on you not to sugar coat anything," he told her as he straightened his vest. "So what's with the dancing? Are you really that bored?"

"Yes, if you must know, I really am that bored."

The prince's smile faded. "I'm sorry. I know you've been here by yourself. I shouldn't tease. May I join you?" He held out his hand. "I didn't know you knew this one. Master Franklin didn't cover it in the autumn."

Lora tentatively took his hand and settled into his arms. "I got tired of the ones I knew. I kept asking him what the drawings on the floor were for, and he finally told me they were for this dance. I made him teach me. He said it was for etiquette in the spring. What is it?"

"It's an old formal dance," Regan explained as he began the steps. "We use it for official events. You know, coronations and royal weddings and the like. I'm told it dates from before Ydris was independent. When we were just a territory in Erasteen."

"So it's Erastinian then," she replied. "It doesn't seem like it. It doesn't seem Ydrisan either. I guess that makes sense. In a weird way." They were quiet for the remainder of the dance. Lora was happy that she only stepped on his feet twice.

Regan bowed and took Lora's arm to lead her out of the etiquette room. "It's good to be back," he said. "You have no idea how dull and how maddening it is to make the decisions that run Ydris."

Lora raised her eyebrows. "Nope, I don't," she agreed. "And I'm glad I never will."

"You'll probably know something like it though," he told her as he pushed his hair out of his eyes. When she gave him a confused look, he continued, "When you marry. Obviously it will be to a lord's son, so you'll have to participate in the local governance."

"No lord's son will marry me," Lora shot back at him. "And certainly not an heir. You forget where I come from, Regan." She sighed and shook her head. "Your highness."

He was quiet for a while. "I think you underestimate what being a swordwielder does to your status, Miss Lorana. You may be of low birth, but a swordwielder is rare. Your husband would be able to use you for any political purpose, which is invaluable. Well, any purpose as long as it doesn't conflict with the king's agenda."

Lora ground her teeth. She tried to pull away from Regan when they got to the swordsplayers' dormitories, but he held fast. "I'd rather marry a commoner than be used in such a way," she declared. "It's bad enough that a husband can dictate so much of his wife's life, but to take her powers and skills?" She made a noise of exasperation, finally wrenched her arm away from him, and stormed inside.

Regan unwisely followed her. "You? Marry a commoner?" The very idea seemed to offend him. "That's preposterous."

She rolled her eyes and bit back a retort. "Well—" She stopped and walked over to her open trunk. "I never leave this open." She scanned the area and tears filled her eyes. Her lovely rose gown was in shreds. She picked up the pieces, tucked them into her arms, let out a sob, and ran from the room.

This time, Regan did not follow.

CHAPTER 14

Lora ran out of the Academy, knowing she was breaking all kinds of rules. She didn't care. She knew it was fruitless, but she had to try. She ran all the way to Mistress Bethany's to see if anything could be done.

"Why Miss Lorana!" Mistress Bethany's smile faded when she took in Lora's tear-stained face and red eyes. "Oh my," she said as she took the pieces of fabric. "What happened?" When Lora shook her head, the tailor's frown deepened. "Well, let's take it to my table. I'll see what I can do."

The dress was in four pieces. It appeared that a knife or a pair of scissors had been used to make holes and the fabric had been ripped apart afterward. The seams looked to have been deliberately avoided.

"Can you fix it?" Lora's voice was small.

Mistress Bethany took a long look at what remained of the dress. "I will do what I can," she said after a moment. "Have you need of anything else?" She took the rest of the young woman in. "You haven't grown any, but you're looking threadbare."

Lora looked at the ground and shrugged. "My cousin has not written to me in months," she admitted.

"I see," Bethany said. "Well, I will help you if it is in my power to do so, young miss. You'd better get back before you're missed. I'll send this over to you when it's finished."

"Thank you." She turned and left. Lora walked very slowly back to the Academy, went straight to her bed in the girl's dormitory, and lay down. It was midafternoon when she got there, and she did not get up for dinner.

She heard footsteps behind her and closed her eyes. "Where did you take it?" Regan asked.

"Bethany's," she replied. "It's the only place I've ever been outside the Academy. I wouldn't know where else to go." She took a deep breath. "This happened while we were dancing. Were you distracting me on purpose so that someone could do this?"

Regan sucked in his breath. "What? No! You can't possibly think that," he said as he turned her toward him. His brow was furrowed and his eyes were earnest. His hair flopped down, and he let go of her to push it back. "You are my friend. I would never do that. I can't believe you would think that."

Lora sat up in a flash. "I don't know what to think!" she hissed. "All I know is that it's very likely I will have one fewer item of clothing to my name. I rely on my cousins for everything, and I haven't heard from either of them since classes began in the fall. I have written six letters between the two of them. You know my situation—everyone does! Look at me! It's obvious everything they do they do because they feel they have to. Even though these dresses are nicer than anything I had back home, they remind me daily that I am so far beneath everyone here..." She took a deep breath and looked the prince right in the eye. "Get out! Just get out!"

His eyes widened in surprise. It's quite possible no one had ever spoken to him that way before, but he turned and left without another word. Lora's face crumpled, she turned, fell onto the bed, and just let the sobs come.

When classes began again a couple of days later, Lora couldn't even get excited about the fact that she was only two assignments behind the rest of her class in literature. Mistress Flora beamed at her as she handed over the novel, but Lora could not smile back. At the end of class, she kept her behind.

"I thought you'd be pleased at the progress you've made," her teacher told her as she sat behind her desk. "I can only assume that something is wrong. What's happened? Is it your cousins? Your family?"

Was it? Lora thought. She shook her head. "No, not really," she whispered. She cleared her throat and stared at the floor. "I don't want to talk about it."

Mistress Flora pursed her lips. "Can you talk to your friends? To one of the other teachers? I know you and Lord Cedric have gotten close. He's spoken of your discourse on a number of occasions. Says you bring a fresh eye to the situations you discuss."

"No, I can't talk to him about this." Lora knew she was being stubborn. She knew Mistress Flora was a younger daughter of one of the border lords, so she would think her despair over losing her dress frivolous. She would not understand what it was like to have her whole life dependent on people who would as soon forget her. "I can't talk to my friends either." She had spoken to no one since she had shouted at Regan. It had made things awkward in the dorms and at meals. Princess Sylvane looked so smug about it. Lora knew she had to have been behind it.

"I'm sorry that you think so," Mistress Flora said. "They'd be poor friends if that were true. " She took a deep breath. "You'd better hurry along. Mistress Diane won't forgive you easily if you're much later. I will speak to her, but don't dawdle."

Lora nodded, gave a small curtsy, and hurried from the room. She slid into her seat as Mistress Diane was introducing a couple of new students in their age group who'd come to the Academy. The

Academy was interesting in that people came at nearly any age to learn, and many left before their training was fully completed. It wasn't necessary for a young noble to be a fully trained swordsplayer to run his lands or serve in her father's guard. Wielders tended to arrive earlier and stay longer, but that was not always the case.

The rest of the morning flew by in a blur. Lora barely tasted her lunch and she rushed to the dorms so she could change without feeling awkward in front of Catty. She was unbuttoning the wine colored dress when she noticed a parcel on her bed. She picked it up warily, as she could not trust that it wasn't from or tampered with by Sylvane. She untied the string holding it closed, and opened up the stuff brown paper. Her breath caught when she saw what was inside.

Before she took out the contents, she read the accompanying note:

Miss Lorana,

I had a note from your cousin, Lady Tiana, the day after we last spoke. She bade me to supply you with some new garments for the spring and included instruction that you were to have

replacements whenever you need. Evidently, she did not want you

waiting for her to appear all the while walking about wearing

dilapidated dresses. I took the liberty of using your old measurements

when I had these made. Have them sent back if they do not fit.

Mistress Bethany

Lora tossed the note aside and lifted her new dresses out. Four everyday dresses in burgundy, emerald green, navy blue, and a deep purple in soft fabric were laid out on her bed. Her hands trembled as she took out the dinner dress. It was a pale blue gown with layers of shimmery fabric pattered with delicate embroidery. It was as nice as anything any of the other girls wore. All of the dresses were.

"It's a pretty dress," Catty said from beside her.

She jumped. "You startled me," Lora said. "I didn't know you'd come in."

Catty snorted. "Obviously." She moved in closer to inspect Lora's new clothes. "So Lady Tiana finally came through. I'm glad. It's so scandalous the way she dresses you." She pressed a lock into her friend's hand. "Regan told me what happened," she said. "I don't want it to happen again. You should be able to lock up your things."

Lora turned and crushed her friend in a hug. "Thank you," she said, Catty's hair muffling her voice. She pulled away and began to get dressed. "And I'm sorry I've been ignoring you all. I just felt so wretched. And I yelled at Regan. I'm sure he'll never forgive me. The way I spoke, I'm lucky I wasn't whipped or locked in the dungeon."

"He told us," Catty laughed. "He said he deserved it. He wouldn't come clean about what you were arguing about though."

Pulling her tunic over her head, Lora raised an eyebrow. "He didn't?" When Catty shook her head, Lora frowned. "I don't know why not. I was ranting about my cousins. They've been ignoring me. I got a little carried away about it."

"Well, he doesn't seem ruffled by it." She tossed her nut brown braid over her shoulder and straightened her tunic. "Anyway, we should get going. I heard we start fighting on horseback today. It might just be a rumor though." She made a face. "Or not. The class above us are supposedly jousting today."

"Jousting? Isn't that kind of a waste of time?"

Catty nodded. "It kind of is. No one really fights like that except when the cavalry charges at the beginning of a battle, but it's exciting. There are always games in Glimmen and the larger cities, like Azure Shores. Next year, when we can go into the city, maybe we'll see one." She smiled. "Perhaps one of the contestants will take your ribbon as a favor and wear it in the tournament." She pretended to swoon and laughed as she stumbled.

CHAPTER 15

It turned out, Catty was wrong. They were learning a new skill on horseback though—riding with no hands, which was the first step in being able to fight with swords or another weapon while on horseback. Plenty of people fell. Sylvane fell three times. Lora couldn't laugh too hard at her though, as she fell twice.

In unarmed combat, Peter landed a blow to Lora's face that had her nose gushing blood. He was mortified, especially as Master Karl seemed impressed he'd landed such a blow and irritated that Lora had let her defenses down. He waved at them, indicating they should carry on with their sparring, and told Lora she could see to her nose at dinner. He handed her a pile of snow and walked away.

Weapons was no better. While Lora was passable at throwing knives, the weight and heft of Shaadi throwing stars felt unnatural to her. She counted herself lucky to hit the target at all and breathed a sigh of relief when she hit the outer ring a couple of times. Lord Sebastian, wincing when he saw the state of her nose, let Lora go a few moments early so that she could see the healers.

Lora was happy to see Genea when she got there. Her friend led her to a cot in a large room and had her sit. She gently sponged what was left of the blood off Lora's face and giggled when she heard that Peter had done it. She sobered again when the healer appeared.

"Now Genea," the healer began. "You know healing is essence wielding. You have to open yourself up to it, unlike the other elements where you grab for it. And you can't just point and direct your power, you have to understand the anatomy and how it is disturbed by how the blow or illness are affecting it."

The healer and Genea each placed a hand on either side of Lora's nose. Genea's face lit up as the healer did her work. Lora could sense that wielding was happening, but beyond that, she had no idea. All she knew was that healing hurt!

"I see you starting to understand," the healer said with a smile. "Now," her attention turned to Lora, "it was indeed broken. It is fixed. You will still have some bruising and swelling, but the worst is done."

Lora frowned. "If you healed me, why do I still have bruising and swelling?"

The healer chuckled. "I could heal you the rest of the way, but it would be for your vanity only. A broken nose can be a liability in a battle. If your opponent knows you have a weakness, he or she can exploit it. A bruise is nothing. We healers also are fallible. We tire. It's best to heal the big stuff and let nature take care of the rest." She then shooed the girls away toward dinner.

Catty, Lora, and Genea bathed and quickly changed in their respective dormitories and raced toward the dining hall. As they ran, Lora smiled at the memory of Lord Allistair telling her that ladies didn't run. Of course, the ladies he knew weren't Academy-trained. When they got there, they found their friends waiting outside. Dain was absent, of course, but a new boy stood with the others. He had a familiar face, but Lora couldn't place his name. It was his shock of bright red hair that tickled at her memory.

"Good to see you out and about, Master Louis," Catty said as she offered her hand. He took it and placed a quick kiss on the back of it. "You weren't too good for us last year. Now that you're able to leave the grounds, you can't be bothered?"

"I've been able to leave the grounds for a year and it's never stopped me from spending time with the group." Regan frowned at Louis. Lora guessed the two were often at odds.

Louis bowed to Lora. "We haven't been formally introduced," he said as he straightened up. "Louis of High Hill, at your service. You must be Lorana, the other swordwielder."

Recognition flooded Lora. She gave a small curtsy and gave him her hand, all too aware of her bitten down nails. "Will I see you in classes then if you're calling yourself a swordwielder?"

He shrugged. "Maybe. They tell me I should, but... If you saw my skill with air, you'd understand." Louis smiled and offered his arm. Lora took it and they followed Catty and Regan into the hall with Peter and Genea trailing behind them.

"Your dress suits you, Lora," Peter told her as the group was settling into their usual table.

She flushed. "Thank you," Lora replied. She busied herself with a roll and began furiously buttering it. "It's new."

"It looks like Sylvane is having apoplexy over there," Catty gestured. "I wonder what's gotten her so upset."

"I wish I knew," Lora put in. She knew it had to be her dress, and Sylvane's reaction confirmed her suspicions that the princess had been behind her old dress's destruction. Well, she certainly didn't want to take advantage of Lord Allistair's sudden generosity, but since she was able to replenish her wardrobe on an as needed basis, the threat of losing something wasn't as dire.

The next few sevendays were fairly boring. True to his word, Louis began to attend their swordwielding independent study lessons. Even though his ability was limited, he was very adept at its use.

"I use it during weapons," he confessed when she asked him about it one evening after class. "I'm not supposed to, since that's for more advanced students, but I don't lose as often as when I don't use it."

Lora nodded. Her potential was great, she was told, but she still had done little more than set drapes on fire and knock things down with air bursts she did not realize she was creating. She had yet to really do more than just sense the other elements. "Are you going to try to create illusions like Lord Michael and Lord Robert want you to?"

Louis shrugged. "I don't like wielding," he admitted. "The only reason I even have lessons is because I'm technically a swordwielder. If I'd come to study wielding, they'd have made sure I didn't suffocate myself or anyone else with air and then sent me on my way. It seems a waste of time."

"If it was a waste of time, you wouldn't be able to use your air as a shield," Lora pointed out. "And our teachers wouldn't think you could do more."

He shrugged again and offered her his arm. "I keep forgetting," he said sheepishly. "Nobody else goes around like this except our group. We're not really expected to until we're adults. I guess it's good practice."

"Maybe," Lora replied. She figured to take advantage of it while it lasted. None of the men in her village led the women around like this, except maybe to and from a dance or if they were courting.

The rest of the term passed quickly. Lora grew to like the sword more and more and got better and better at throwing knives. She continued to excel at archery and enjoyed the one area where she received praise. She continued to struggle with wielding, but was at least able to begin sensing the other elements more consistently. Louis continued to come to swordwielding, but he left frustrated and angry more often than not. He was always more grouchy in general on days where he was required to go to wielding classes of any kind. While Lora would have like to have a confidante in him as she had in Dain, she didn't think that was going to happen.

On the last day of classes before the summer holidays, Mistress Flora handed out their summer assignments. "Now, all of you are going to be reading this work by Lord Philbert of James Lake. It's an old treatise of the war with Korlisse that was going on about two hundred years ago. The language is a little different than what we speak today, but you all should be fine with it especially considering you have several months to finish." She nodded to her assistant to begin handing out the books. "I'll expect an essay, three to four parchments long, on some aspect of the book you find interesting. You will be expected to use outside sources to substantiate your views. At least two."

Lora was not paying attention. Mistress Flora always gave her assignments after classes ended. She picked up the book the assistant handed her when classes were dismissed and walked over to her teacher. "What will my summer assignment be, Mistress Flora?"

"You weren't paying attention," she said. It was not a question.

"I didn't think I needed to, since I won't be reading what they're reading," Lora replied, suddenly feeling awkward. She didn't like admitting to not paying attention.

Mistress Flora smiled. "I did say *all* of you would be reading the book, Lora."

"All of us. Including me." When Mistress Flora nodded, she continued, "The same book. At the same time. Together."

"Yes," Mistress Flora laughed. "You've caught up to the rest of the class. It's time for you to join in on the same assignments. Maybe start paying attention in class, hmmm?"

Lora blushed. "I can't believe it."

"Believe it," her teacher told her. "You've been pushed hard over the past two years and you've worked even harder. You've actually worked harder than any student I've ever seen here. In fact, I probably could have put you on the same assignment sooner, but I didn't want to overwhelm you." She paused. "The other teachers have commented on you, too, Lora. We're all really pleased."

She swallowed. "Do you think that if I keep it up, I could be above the average? Smart even?"

"Lora, I already think you're smart," Mistress Flora said, patting her student on the cheek. "You've just been at a disadvantage." She smiled. "Go on now. You'll be late for Mistress Diane. I'll see you around. Come to me with any questions."

Lora nodded and walked out of the classroom. It was unbelievable. Had she really caught up to her classmates? She pondered the question for the rest of the day.

At dinner, the mood shifted between subdued and excited. Everyone was glad to be going on their various summer adventures, but they were all sad to be saying goodbye to each other.

"Lora, are you stuck here again all summer?" Louis asked. When she nodded, he whistled. "There's got to be some way to get you out of here for a while."

Catty nodded. "My father said you could come to Arbor Cove. You can share the carriage with me. He said he wrote to your cousins and they didn't forbid it exactly. They just said they weren't supporting you there if you chose to go."

"Or if you prefer to stay, I'll be here all summer," Genea put in.

"As will I," the prince added. "I'm sure we can think of loads of things to do that will keep us in trouble."

Lora laughed at her friends' generosity. "I thank you all. It's very nice of you to include me, but I'll be staying here," she said. She made eye contact with Catty. "I worry that if I go anywhere, my cousin will stop paying my board here during that time and forget to start paying it again."

"Gallivanting about Glimmen it is!" Genea cheered.

There actually wasn't much gallivanting going on that summer. Genea and Lora met at least once a sevenday and shared a meal together, half of which were at the Academy and the other half at Genea's father's house. Lora thought the whole of the Haven Dale keep would fit inside it with room to spare.

Regan was true to his word and visited with Lora about half the times that Genea was there. King Gerald had kept him awfully busy since his seventeenth birthday, which was early in the spring, so they were glad to see him whenever they could. They spoke of

anything and everything, sometimes practiced swordsplay, discussed
Mistress Flora's assignment, and tried to stay on top of their studies.

Lora enjoyed all of the visits. She wasn't nearly as lonely as
she had been on any other holiday break. She was included in gossip,
minor intrigues, and other things she had always missed out on
before. She was nearly giddy with delight.

She was surprised when Lady Tiana paid her a visit. Lora was
relieved when she didn't ask her about her attire. It was nearing the
end of summer and everything was too short and threadbare.

Tiana grabbed Lora's hand and inspected it. "Still being bitten,
but not as badly," she mused. "Well, I suppose it's a start." She looked
her up and down. "You've grown. And you're starting to get breasts. I
suppose you'll need new clothes then. Have your courses arrived?"
When Lora shook her head, she sighed. "Very well. Let's go."

Lora blushed bright red. She was mortified. It seemed that
Lady Tiana was obsessed with women's troubles and intimate
activities, since she brought it up at every meeting. Lora had hoped to

go dress shopping alone just prior to the start of the school year so she was a little disappointed to be going with her. There were still a couple of sevendays to go, which was fine, but she would have liked to go to Mistress Bethany's on her own.

The walk to the tailor was short and Mistress Bethany greeted them cheerfully when they entered. She inquired about Lady Tiana's marriage, and Lady Tiana inquired about hers. Lora supposed that was polite conversation for adults. She hadn't really paid much attention before.

"Well, Mistress Bethany, I wish we were here for small talk," Tiana explained. "It's time for Cousin Lorana to have some new dresses. As you can see, she's grown and her womanly curves are upon her. She will need suitable underthings, more adult-style gowns, and some undergarments for when she begins her courses. You think that will be soon since she's gotten hips and breasts now?"

Lora had not thought her face could flame any redder, but she had been mistaken. Mistress Bethany gave an awkward glance toward Lora and cleared her throat. "I have three daughters, and in my experience, yes Lady Tiana. That is usually when they come. You're right in being as prepared as possible."

Tiana nodded. "Excellent. Well, plain styles again. Perhaps we might increase the quality of fabric we're using, especially as regards to her evening dress. Do you have occasion to wear it, Cousin?"

"Yes, often," Lora replied. "We wear eveningwear every night as part of etiquette practice."

"Good," she said. "An excellent habit." Tiana frowned. "She's still too young for a formal gown. I guess that's fortuitous. Next year then."

Lora wandered off. She knew that Lady Tiana would choose the fabrics she wanted whether Lora had an opinion or not. Case in point, the orange nightmare. She shook her head. She'd noticed her body changing, but tried to ignore it. Her friends were much curvier than she was, so she knew it wouldn't draw anyone's attention. Not that she wanted anyone's attention.

Once the order for the dresses was completed, Lady Tiana accompanied Lora back to the Academy. "You'll be needing some pocket money now that you're able to leave the school grounds," she explained. "You will have an allowance of two silvers per month to spend on whatever rubbish you wish. Or you may save it and purchase something larger. You will not receive more than that."

"That is very generous, Cousin Tiana," Lora told her. And it was generous. She had never seen more than two silvers together before. Now she had two silvers in a small purse Lady Tiana provided for her.

"Now, you mind that purse," Tiana said. "There are pickpockets everywhere in this city. If the money is stolen, it will not be replaced. I'm counting on you to be responsible. Oh, I nearly forgot. Your father and brother send their regards. Shall I bring yours back?" Lora nodded, Tiana bid her farewell, and she retired to the dorms.

Lora wished that Lady Tiana would be more specific about what her father and brother were doing. Were they in good health?

Was her father able to do more than his indentured fletching? Was her brother, Shawn, being a help? Shawn would be sixteen. Nearly a man. Was he courting anyone? Gods, was her father? A tear ran down her cheek. It occurred to her that they might have just as many questions about her that went unanswered. She tucked her sadness inside her and began to practice her curtsies.

The parcel with her gowns arrived a sevenday later. Lora had not been paying attention to the ordering, but she couldn't remember Tiana and Mistress Bethany discussing any violet fabric, but there was a violet day dress. She shrugged and figured that either she had not been paying close enough attention to know what was examined and purchased or that Mistress Bethany had been very kind and was helping her to avoid another rancid egg yolk. It could have been either, so Lora just shrugged and moved on.

The underthings had Lora blushing scarlet yet again. They were a woman's undergarments. They were trimmed with a small amount of lace and covered much less skin than she felt they ought to. The items for her monthly courses were perplexing, and she hoped she could ask her friends for help when the time came.

Her friends began arriving shortly after her clothes did. They were full of exciting stories of the things they did and the places they went. Catty had evidently traveled to James Lake with her father while he worked with Lord Brandon, King Gerald's chief advisor.

"He's a windbag," Catty declared. "And his son Geoffrey is not much better. Be glad he isn't here because it would be insufferable."

"Oh come now," Regan put in. "Geoff's not so bad. He's just a little bit sheltered. His father is in Glimmen most of the year and Geoffrey has had the reign of those estates since he was about thirteen. That will puff up anyone's importance. Once he spends more time here, that will change. And he will probably come next year. Our fathers mean for him to be my chief advisor when the time comes." He shrugged and his hair flopped into his face. He was used to a lot of decisions being made on his behalf.

Catty rolled her eyes. "I still say he's a clod. At least Dain was there to save me."

"I wonder what you say about me when I'm not here," Peter said softly.

"Nothing, Peter," Catty said sweetly. "You're sweet, humble, smart, patient..."

"I can't help but notice that handsome was not on that list," Louis pointed out.

"I thought that was obvious," Catty told him. "Why should I have to point out the obvious?" She put her hands on her hips and gave the boys her sternest look. "It's awfully unfair that you are all handsome. Especially because you all know it."

Regan snorted. "Be still my beating heart!" he swooned. "These three lovely ladies think we humble gentlemen are handsome!" He fell out of his chair laughing. They were in the deserted dining hall, but there were still workers present. Several of them gave their group cold looks meant to tell them to show more restraint and decorum.

Genea and Lora blushed and Catty rolled her eyes. Genea cleared her throat, "Well, I assure you that things here in Glimmen were pretty quiet, as Lora and his highness can attest." She felt she had to change the subject. It was far too awkward.

CHAPTER 16

Their last few days before classes began were spent merry-making. They went into Glimmen several times, even though the older students had been doing this for a year or more. The older of the group showed the younger the best places to eat and shop and gave them tips to prevent being pickpocketed. Lora had been dismayed to see the prices of everything. In Haven Dale, things were a fraction of the cost that they were in Glimmen. Her two silvers a month, which had seemed like a huge amount of money, would get her very little.

Once classes began, Lora waited trepidatiously for her essay in literature to be graded. It consumed her thoughts. She was distracted in theory of war, for which Lord Cedric scolded her in front of the entire class. She apologized to him afterward. She received a "humph" for her efforts.

Her distraction got her another broken nose in unarmed combat. Peter was mortified. Again. He would not take the praise from Master Karl and fought vehemently against the chastisement he gave Lora. He walked her to the healer's complex after an argument with Master Karl got him punished.

"Why argue with him?" Lora asked, trying not to swallow the blood dripping down the back of her throat. She wasn't sure what was less ladylike: spitting out blood or swallowing it. Since swallowing it was making her gag, she settled on the former.

He kicked the dirt as they walked. "Because it's not right to punish you for being injured and to praise me for injuring you."

Lora sighed. "You do understand that someday it won't be me that you're sparring with?" she asked. "You won't be yelled at for getting hit. You'll be dead. That's why he gets so upset. I wasn't paying attention. I deserve this. Or worse."

"That doesn't mean I have to like hitting you in the face," Peter pointed out. "I'd much rather punch Regan. Can't hit him when he's king. Kind of fun to do it now. But he's not in our class, so there's pretty limited opportunity for it."

The worst calamity came in horsemanship. They had begun to ride without their hands in the last term, and now they were progressing on. They were given weapons to use while on horseback for the very first time. The first few lessons were spent learning how to hold the various weapons and shields, after which they would learn the differences between fighting on the ground versus fighting on horseback. Ultimately, they would begin fighting each other.

Lord Ian was shouting for them to move different directions in formation while holding their weapons and changing their weapons' positions. Ever since they had been learning to ride using only their knees and posture to control their mounts, there had been many falls. Few injuries, but many falls. Lora turned a little bit too swiftly to the left and down she went.

A run of vulgar expletives came pouring out of her mouth as she held back tears. Lora knew her arm was broken even before she was scooped up by one of her burlier classmates and carried to the healer complex.

"Why Lorana," the healer on duty told her. "You're getting to be quite the frequent customer here. Young man, tell me what happened."

"Riding with weapons," he explained. "She fell off her horse and landed on her arm. She ah…" His ears turned red. "She said some things afterward, and we figured she broke her arm, so Lord Ian told me to bring her here."

The healer smiled and waved over a more advanced student. "Diagnosis?"

"Um… Fracture of the ulna and radius just proximal to the wrist." His hands hovered above Lora's wrist.

"Good, good. Now walk me through the steps of what you will heal and how you will heal it," the older healer said.

Lora did not care to hear about the exact healing process so she closed her eyes. Dried tears made her cheeks feel tight, but her free arm was strapped down so she could not wipe them away. Her classmate had left nearly as soon as he dropped her off, which was just as well. As the healer fixed her arm, an even more colorful stream of curse words erupted from her mouth.

The healer laughed, checked over her student's work, sent him off to write up a report on what he had done, and turned to Lora. "You must've spent a good amount of time around commoners."

"Why do you say that?" Lora asked. The line of conversation was making her very nervous.

"Well, my family is pretty lowly ranked away from the baron who controls the area," she said. "There were commoners in my town that were wealthier than us. I did not have the advantage of proper schooling. My vocabulary is much like yours."

Lora nodded. "It appears that our backgrounds are nearly the same." She took a deep breath and let it out in relief. "I thank you for your services. When can I return to my swordplay courses?"

"At least a sevenday," she explained. She waived off Lora's protests. "Remember, it's not fully healed. We just help it on its way.

I will see you back here then to check your progress—as well as my student's."

She thought she was fortunate to have broken her left hand. At least she could still write and complete her general assignments. Lora trudged back to the dormitory and began changing for dinner. Her wrist and hand ached terribly, but she managed. She was about halfway finished when Catty and Genea came bursting in.

"Why Lora of Haven Dale!" Catty exclaimed. "I didn't know you had it in you. Such language!" She collapsed on her bed and howled with laughter.

"Master Ian, well, everyone said he turned purple when you were shouting," Genea told her as she helped button up Lora's gown. "I'm not sure if it was because he was angry you were swearing or because he was shocked at what you were saying. Or both. I must say, I don't even know what half of what they're saying you said means."

"Of course you wouldn't," a voice from over by the door rang out. Sylvane waltzed into their dorm and flounced on her bed. "No one in polite society, especially a lady, would utter such vulgarity," she said. "I wouldn't be surprised if you got extra duties for it."

Lora paled and then straightened up. There was something about the smug look on Sylvane's face that really got her goat. "Well, princess, there's a lot more where that came from," she said. "Shall I continue?"

Sylvane's mouth formed a perfect O. Her hands covered her face, she squeaked, and she ran from the room.

"I've been wanting to get her to run away from us for a long time," Catty remarked once she got ahold of herself. "I didn't know it would be so easy as offending her with my uncouth vocabulary. Really, Lora, you've been holding back all this time. How do you know such marvelous words and phrases?"

"Well," Lora began. She knew she was in trouble. She thought for a moment before responding. She was treading a fine line between the truth and artifice. "I lived in a small village. I went to the same school as the commoners in Haven Dale. I spent time with them. Evidently I picked up their bad habits and... colorful vocabulary."

Genea smiled. "That makes sense. That or perhaps you spent too much time on board ship, but I know you haven't done that," she teased. "The second best part about this, other than Sylvane's reaction just now, was the boys'. Peter said he about fell off his horse too. I'm sure Regan and Louis will have heard by now. Gods, I bet the whole Academy has heard!"

Lora groaned and hid her face in her hands. "I wish there was a way for dinner to come to me in here until this blows over."

"You'll be waiting a long time for that," Catty told her.

A few hours later in Lord Ian's chambers, a group of teachers gathered. "Did she really?" Lord Cedric asked. "She's such a little thing. Her manners are a little coarse, but I can hardly believe it."

Lord Ian nodded. "I can hardly believe it myself. I'm not sure what to do about it either. Breaking her wrist is punishment enough for being distracted. But, I'm vacillating on her language. Part of me thinks it's hilarious. The other half knows that a young lady should never utter such uncouth words."

Master Franklin held up his finger. "If I may interrupt," he interjected. "As the sole representative here who is responsible for teaching etiquette, I believe my opinion to be quite relevant." He cleared his throat. "Her exclamation upon breaking her arm is quite expected. It's the nature of it that's in question. What, may I ask, would you have had her say instead? 'Oh drat?' As refined as I believe myself to be, I know I would have said something similar."

"Not like this," Lord Ian muttered.

CHAPTER 17

The Incident of the Oaths, as it came to be called, was the talk of the Academy for the next sevenday. Lora had no further mishaps. She learned her lessons. Her marks were on her mind, but she pushed them to the side when she was in class. At the end of her sevenday of no swordsplay, the literature essays were handed back to them. Lora was delighted to see average marks, especially when Catty and Genea received similar. No one could have been happier to be average.

Lora's happiness was short lived that day. When she was changing after weapons, she noticed some blood. She knew what it was, but she panicked all the same. "Catty!" she called.

"What?" she replied. "Hurry up and get dressed or we won't have time to eat, and I'm starving!"

"I need your help," she said. Lora took a deep breath and placed her hand on the wall of the privy they all shared. "I have my courses. I need my things, and... I need help using them. I don't know how."

There was a pause. "Of course. I'll be right back."

Catty was true to her word and returned in a matter of moments. Lora let her into the small cubicle and to Lora's mortification, insisted on showing her exactly how to use her special undergarments instead of telling her like she would have preferred. "Didn't your mother tell you about these things?"

Lora shook her head. "No, she died when I was five, and Lady Tiana only insisted these be included with my new gowns. She didn't say anything about how they were to be used." She looked down at her hands. "Thank you for helping me, Catty."

"What are friends for?" she said with a shrug. "You're one of us now," she swooned and laughed. "Womanhood. It's not all it's cracked up to be." She paused. "Did anyone tell you about... You know. How babies come about."

"Yes," she replied. "Some of them women in the village made mention of it," Lora's face turned crimson. "Lady Tiana said something too. Just 'relations are for the marriage bed,' and that if I don't follow that, this whole endeavor would be a waste of Cousin Allistair's time and money if I got a bastard in my belly."

Catty wiggled her eyebrows, her grin widening. "That's no fun," she said. "There are pregnancy charms and potions for preventing that from happening, you know."

Lora frowned. "I haven't even kissed a boy," she said. "I'm not interested and neither are they."

"Oh, but kissing is so much fun," Catty exclaimed. "It wouldn't take much more to go beyond that." She shrugged. "I like kissing."

"Who? I thought you would've told me about something like this!"

"I can't kiss and tell, but you do know one of them. The rest are down in Arbor Cove."

She was aghast. "There's been more than one?"

Catty smiled coyly. "As well there should be," she replied. "You can't very well marry some stodgy old dolt until you've lived a little now, can you?"

"I can't," Lora said. "I'm a poor choice for any marriage made here. Or anywhere. Relations, and kissing I guess, would only lower me further."

"Lora, you talk like kissing and a roll in the hay are things you can decide to say no to far in advance," Catty said. "Your emotions and your heart aren't so black and white." She paused. "You really don't like anyone?"

"It would be a waste of my time," Lora replied. "So no. I won't look at anyone like that. When I'm done here, I'll do my duty to the kingdom, go back to my village, or one like it, and marry someone there."

Catty tapped her lips thoughtfully. "Peter likes you," she said. "I bet he'd kiss you."

"That's ridiculous. You're ridiculous." Lora crossed her arms in front of her chest and began to walk out. "Even if it wasn't, I don't like him. So please stop."

"You're no fun, Lora!" Catty called. She giggled and ran after her friend. They were late for dinner, and the boys would be cross for making them wait.

Lora spent most of the rest of autumn term staring at Peter trying to decide if he liked her. He never seemed to be watching her while she watched him, so she doubted it. Unless he was watching her while she was looking away. How would she know he was watching her if she was looking away? These thoughts plagued her mind day in and day out. And Catty teased her relentlessly about it. Lora wasn't sure why. She didn't like Peter like that. He was a friend. He'd broken her nose twice. She just wanted to know if her friend's assumptions were true, and she got nowhere closer to knowing the answer.

CHAPTER 18

A tournament was announced for a couple of sevendays after the equinox. The entire Academy, including the teachers, was abuzz in anticipation. The first and second year students all lamented that they couldn't attend, and it was all the older students could talk about. Everyone was going.

"Regan, swordwielders can't participate, can they?" Peter was asking.

The prince shook his head, sending his blond hair flying. "Not in the general events. There's too great a risk of cheating, even accidentally. If the tournament is big enough, sometimes there will be an event or two just for them. But this tournament is pretty small as far as they go. The one in the summer is bigger. So is the spring tournament in Azure Shores."

"They haven't published the lists, have they?" Catty asked as she twirled a lock of her dark brown hair around her finger.

"Not exactly," Regan was saying. "But since the crown is the main patron, I know who's going to be participating."

Lora continued to eat her dinner. Haven Dale was too small for anything but the odd archery tournament. She had nothing meaningful to contribute to the conversation. And unlike everyone else, she wasn't sure if she was even going. It cost three silvers to sit where her friends wanted to, and she had only saved four since the term had begun. The other would surely go to food and drink, and she had been hoping to get some small gift for Catty for midwinter.

"And?" Genea squealed. She hid her blush behind her curly black hair. Young ladies did not squeal.

Louis nudged Regan. "You can tell us. At least a couple of the big names."

Regan rolled his eyes. "Fine. First of all, there's going to be a display done by some of the wielders. That'll be something different. I guess Lord Michael has something planned. Lord Jeremy will be doing something too. Phillip, Dain's brother, will be in the mêlée. Lord Harrison is supposed to be jousting. Master Karl will be wrestling. There's no one you'd know in the projectile competitions." When Lora snapped out of her reverie, the prince smiled. "Yes, Lora. There's an archery competition. Perhaps you could give them some pointers? I've heard you're practically the best in the Academy."

"I doubt that," Lora said with a snort.

"You never give yourself any credit, Lora," Catty chided. "It's too bad you can't do the competition since you're a swordwielder. I bet your air talent would make your arrows soar straighter and farther than anyone else's."

Peter grinned. "She doesn't even need that. She's better than anyone in our class or the classes below us for sure. Like Regan said, probably the best at the Academy."

Lora scowled. "It's not like I can shoot an apple off anyone's head. And I certainly wouldn't try it."

"In any case," Regan cut in, "next rest day, we will get to see all of these dazzling feats and more at the tournament."

Louis raised his eyebrow mischievously. "Do you think anyone will be maimed or killed?"

"That's so morbid, Louis," Genea told him. "No one hopes for that. At lease, I hope they don't."

"Of course they do," Louis replied as he ran his hand through his thick red hair. "The blood and gore are half the point of going."

In the end, Louis made Genea cry and Regan made him apologize. Lora wasn't sure what to expect after that. She awaited the tourney with as much anticipation as anyone.

On the morning of the tournament, the girls awoke early so as not to miss any of the events. The jousts would last all day with the champion to be decided at sundown. The projectile competitions were to be held in the hours around noon. The mêlée would be mid-morning, and the wrestling matches in the afternoon. The wielder displays would also be going on for most of the day and into the evening. The group would be hard pressed to see everything they wanted to.

After much discussion, the girls decided they would wear their everyday dresses and not something fancier. There hadn't been enough time to have a nicer day dress made for any of them, and eveningwear was out of the question on a dusty tourney field. They just imagined that they would be dressed as glamorously as the adult women in attendance.

"I've talked my mother and father out of forcing me to stay in their box with them, so I'll be able to be with the group," Regan was saying as they walked toward the tourney grounds, which Lora had unknowingly passed by on her journey into Glimmen. "I'll have to break away for the final joust though."

Catty made a face. "Sometimes I forget you're the prince and you have all of these silly responsibilities," she said. "I mean, I'm glad you fulfill them, but it doesn't leave room for a lot of fun."

"Uncle Gerald says there's nothing fun about running a kingdom," Genea put in. "It can be rewarding, but it's almost never fun."

When they reached their destination, they got a program and planned out their day. Lord Harrison wasn't jousting until after the mêlée was supposed to be over, so they were excited that they would be able to see him as well as Dain's brother. Most of the group wanted to see the wielder demonstrations over a leisurely lunch, but Lora obviously wanted to watch the archery. She said nothing while the group was making plans, and resolved to go on her own. They would watch Master Karl and finish out the day at the joust and more wielder demonstrations. The firewielders were going to show their skills after dark.

They headed over to the lists to watch the jousting for a while before the mêlée. Regan had secured them a box that they all pitched in to pay for. It was halfway between the royal box and the starting point for the combatants, so it had a good view of where the opponents would collide.

Jousting bored Lora as a general rule, but there was something about the jousting at the tourney. All the crashing and bashing and exploding of lances and the bright colors. She was hooked. Regan teased her unmercifully.

"Fine," she said, waving him off. "It's exciting and I'm enjoying watching it. That doesn't mean that I have to like doing it myself. Or that I'll enjoy the archery any less. Archery is so different. Quiet. The precision and the skill make it exciting in a different way."

Regan laughed. "Then I'll have to escort you when it's time for the shooting of the arrows," he told her. He flashed her a grin and pointed to where the current opponents were having it out with swords after they had failed to unseat each other after three passes. "And when the lances fail, it's even better than the mêlée. "

"I wouldn't go that far," Louis shouted over the din. "Still better than arrows though. Sorry Lora."

"Can't win 'em all!" Lora shouted back at him.

After one more pair of jousters had their turn, the group went to the stadium and found a spot to watch the mêlée from. The mêlée in this tourney would be fought on foot, as opposed to others which began on horseback. Catty spotted Dain's brother, who wore their house colors and arms on his shield. Lora surprised herself by recognizing several sigils. Master Franklin's classes were paying off, evidently.

Two groups of fighters gathered in loose formations on either side of the stadium. They stood poised and ready for action. A bugler sounded and the chaos began. The groups ran at each other, screaming and yelling and waving their weapons. The sound when they crashed together was deafening. Even with blunted and lightened weapons, injuries seemed common. Blood littered the ground. Lora, who had never seen anything like this, began to feel sick. *This is what my life will be?* she thought.

After what seemed like hours, four fighters were left. Three from one group and one from the other. The three surrounded their opponent and attacked him all at once. Two fell to sword strokes that seemed faster than lightening. It was now one on one. The larger of the two feinted and charged in when the other parried. The larger man slipped and the smaller clipped his helmet sending him to the ground. The mêlée was over.

"Well, that was surprising," Genea mused. "Lord Bertrand overcame three to one odds to pull it off in the end. Even with twenty years on Master Lorne."

Lora took a deep breath and swallowed. That was the worst thing she had ever seen, and she knew it did not compare to the gore and violence of a real battle in war. She knew as a swordwielder that most of the time she would be away from the main fighting, but when she was in the thick of it, would she be able to do what was needed?

She rose and snuck away from her friends who were gesturing wildly and talking excitedly and animatedly about what they had just seen. Lora passed by some of the food vendors and balked when she saw what they were asking for even the simplest fare. It appeared she would be going hungry that day.

Easily finding the archery set up, she climbed up the small grandstand and found herself a seat that was unobtrusive and out of the way. There were one hundred archers in the competition and they would go in groups of ten starting at fifty paces. The distance between the arrows to the center of the targets would be carefully measured, and the top fifty archers would move on. The next distance would be seventy five paces and the twenty closest to the bull's eye would move on. At one hundred paces, the ten best would move on to two hundred paces, and the winner would be chosen from there. If a tie occurred, the final archers would shoot at that distance until a winner was declared. Archers would use their own bows and arrows so that no one would have an advantage or disadvantage over using unfamiliar equipment.

Lora had been considered a fair archer before she had come to Glimmen. There were others in Haven Dale who had been better, and she was glad to see that none of them were there to recognize her. She looked at the competitors with interest and was surprised to see more commoners in the contest than nobles. Of course, archery was not considered suitable to the nobility unless it was something they had taken up at the Academy. Although, she had heard Lord Allistair had a fair hand with the longbow. She looked a little more carefully and smiled when she picked him out. At least she'd have someone to cheer for.

The distance of fifty paces was the longest and most boring by far. One hundred distances needed to be measured, and at that close range, they really all should have been in the center circle. There were many flushes of embarrassment when the second, and even the third circle from the center, were pierced. Lora was pleased to see Lord Allistair move on to seventy five paces and clapped heartily when his name was announced. The wind picked up a little bit for this round and she was excited to see how that would affect their aim. Wind was considered to be the great equalizer in archery. If one could correct for it, they were probably pretty good.

Lord Allistair was twenty fourth, and so did not move on to the round at one hundred paces. Lora was disappointed, but not surprised. He had looked a little peeved at the wind, which generally meant he didn't want to deal with it. She thought he let his attitude affect his abilities, and archery required too much mental discipline for him to overcome it.

The rest of the contest went by quickly, and a young man from Peter's home eventually took the win. Lora made a mental note to congratulate Peter on Lone Pine's victory. She rose from her position in the stands and went down to congratulate Lord Allistair. She found him laughing with a couple of men near his own age and stood off to the side waiting for an opportunity to speak.

The Lord of Haven Dale's eyes brushed over her and he started. "Cousin?" he choked. "Is that you?"

Lora smiled and bobbed a small curtsy of greeting that one cousin would make to another. "Cousin Allistair, what an unexpected pleasure to see you compete today!" she exclaimed. "You have done our home proud, I should say."

He bowed awkwardly. "Gentlemen, this is my cousin, Miss Lorana," Allistair said. "Cousin, this is Master Charles of Windy Heath and Lord Thomas of Green Meadows. Charles is my lady wife's brother."

"Very pleased to meet you both," she told them.

"Lorana is a swordwielder studying at the Academy," Lord Allistair explained. "I am sponsoring her." He turned to her and frowned. "You did not come to the tourney alone, I hope."

Lora shook her head. "No, Cousin. I came with a group of friends. I was the only one who wanted to watch archery, so we parted after the mêlée. I'm to meet them at the wrestling area in a moment. I just wanted to congratulate you on placing so well."

Allistair smiled. "Thank you," he said. "You have changed, Cousin."

"It's been over two years," she laughed. "I certainly hope so!"

"Get along with you now," he gestured, suddenly impatient to get back to his friends. "Go find your friends and enjoy the rest of the day."

She curtsied and began to walk away. She stopped when she heard Lord Thomas quip, "A swordwielder! I'm jealous of the prestige she'll bring to your family. Shame she's so homely though."

Lora felt tears sting her eyes and she hurried away to find her friends. She knew she wasn't anywhere near as pretty as her friends, but to hear it like that hurt. A lot. She wiped her eyes and cheeks when she saw her group standing together and took a deep breath. She knew it was too much to hope that no one would notice.

And she was right. Regan and Catty frowned when they saw her. The prince opened his mouth to say something and Lora waved him off. "My cousin was twenty fourth in the archery contest," she said, managing a shaky smile. "Peter, a commoner from your estate won. You should be proud."

Catty's frown deepened. "Your cousin? I assume you spoke with him afterward then."

Lora looked away and pointed to a good spot that could accommodate everyone in their group. "Let's hurry and claim that before anyone else does." She moved away from Catty to walk in next to Peter, who was always oblivious and would say nothing to her about the state she was in. She knew she couldn't escape for long, but she hoped she would be able to fully compose herself before that happened.

Peter looked at her and reached into his pocket and pulled something out of it. "I wasn't sure if you would have enough coin to get something to eat," he said quietly. "I got this for you." He held out a slightly flattened meat pie.

"Oh, thank you Peter, but—" Lora's stomach betrayed her and she winced. "Thank you." She took the pie from him and began to eat it as they walked. "That was very thoughtful of you."

He shrugged. "I know you'd never say anything, so I took the initiative. I'm glad your stomach gave you away. I know you wouldn't have accepted it otherwise." He smiled and sat in the row behind her with Louis.

Lora felt, rather than saw, Catty sit on one side of her and Regan on the other. "What happened?" Catty demanded.

"What did your cousin say that upset you so much?" Regan asked at almost the same time.

"My cousin said nothing," she said with a sigh. "I overheard his companion say something as I walked away. I'm over it now. Don't worry about it. Please."

It was fortunate that the bugle announced the start of the wrestling at that moment. Lora had a hard time getting into it, since her thoughts were elsewhere. She spent most of her time trying to get by unnoticed, and someone had gone and noticed her—and not for any good reason. She certainly knew her looks left something to be desired. She'd never been a pretty child and never had aspirations of beauty. It wasn't worth wanting something that would never happen. But no one had ever gone and described her for what she was. It hurt. It hurt more than she had imagined it would.

All too quickly, the wrestling was over. Lora had no idea who had won or how well Master Karl had done. She hoped no one would try and talk to her about it. She took the arm Louis offered and walked with him over to their box overlooking the lists. Lora was glad he was absorbed in conversation with Peter and Genea. She was not in the mood to talk.

She did not enjoy the rest of the tournament. She did not shout with the rest of her companions when Lord Harrison was unhorsed. She did not partake in dinner, even when Catty brought her a meat pie and set it in front of her. She did not ooh and ah at the wielder displays that went on until after full dark. She was glad to walk off the tourney grounds and back into the swordsplayer girls' dormitory.

"Alright, Lora," Catty said after they changed into their nightgowns. "What gives? I left you alone and made Regan leave you alone too. Now it's just you and me. You can tell me. What happened?"

Lora sighed and got under her covers. "I'm ugly," she whispered. And there it was.

Catty frowned. "That's ridiculous. I won't have anyone saying that about my friend, no matter who they are."

"It's only ridiculous because you're my friend," Lora said, turning away from her. "I've always known I was no prize, but I've never heard it put quite like that before. So never you mind, Catty.

Just let it be." She paused. "And don't tell Regan. He wouldn't

understand."

CHAPTER 19

On the second to last day of classes, Lora was furiously taking notes in theory of war when Catty nudged her with her elbow. Lora frowned and elbowed her back. She liked to make sure she heard every word Lord Cedric said to the class. His tests were notoriously difficult, and she was determined not to miss anything.

Catty nudged her again. "Guess what," she whispered out of the corner of her mouth.

Lora ignored her and continued to write.

"You'll never guess."

"Then I guess it can wait until after class," Lora replied.

"You're no fun," Catty pouted. "I guess I'll tell you anyway. I'm not going to Arbor Cove for the winter holidays." She waited for a response and frowned when Lora continued to write. "I'll be staying at school."

Lora gave a tiny smile. "Wonderful. We can make plans over lunch."

Catty raised her eyes to the ceiling and muttered a prayer to the gods. "Don't you want to know why?"

"Miss Catherine," came Lord Cedric's booming voice. "Do you have a question? Something you'd like to share with the class?" The rest of the class being the approximately three hundred fifty swordsplay and wielder students who were currently enrolled at the Academy. He waited for her to speak for a full minute. "No? Then I would hope you would do us all the courtesy of waiting until the end of class to share whatever news you have for Miss Lorana. And yes. I can hear everything you're saying. Wonderful thing to be in a place full of such clever wielders. The acoustics in this hall are just marvelous." He smiled and turned back to his blackboard.

Catty took copious notes through the end of class. She was semi-mortified. Whenever Lord Cedric scolded anyone, it became the hot subject of discussion at the Academy for at least a sevenday. You gained notoriety. Not necessarily the sort you wanted, but you definitely became a talked about figure.

When Lord Cedric called the end of class, Lora stretched and yawned. "Yes? You were saying?"

"You're impossible," she groaned. "Anyway, I'll be staying here. I've been invited to the big midwinter ball at the palace." She grinned and twirled around as they stepped into the courtyard at the entrance to the large lecture hall where theory of war was held.

Lora stopped walking and turned back toward her friend. "But you won't be sixteen until the spring. How can you go?"

"I was invited, and no one's kicking up a fuss. It appears either no one has noticed that I'm still fifteen. Or no one cares."

"I wonder if Regan will invite me next year." Even if she were invited, Lora did not want to go. She was awkward enough in day to day settings with nobles. Adding in a fancy ball where strict etiquette rules applied was just asking for disaster.

Catty giggled. "Of course he will. He's our friend."

"Has he invited Louis and Peter?"

"Why are you asking about Peter?" she teased.

Lora crossed her arms in front of her chest as they walked into the dormitory together. "I'm asking because if Regan's asking out of friendship, everyone we know who can go will have been asked. That includes Peter, Louis, and you." She grinned evilly. "If he only asked you, he might be asking for a kiss. Or more. He is starting to get quite the reputation."

Catty stepped out of her dress. "I hadn't thought of that," she admitted. Her eyes narrowed. "What have you heard?"

"What haven't I heard?" Lora replied. She tried and failed to sound innocent. "Alright, alright. I heard a few girls from his class complaining about him. Kisses and promises, promises broken. More than kisses, evidently for one poor girl. Lots of talk of pregnancy potions with that story."

"He's insufferable." Catty tugged on her tunic and continued to scowl.

Lora pulled her leggings up under her tunic. "He's the prince. He can do whatever he wants and people will turn the other way nearly every time."

"That's disgusting," Catty declared. "Especially considering if he's this free with the girls at the Academy, think about the common ones. There'll be three times as many of them." She ran a comb through her hair and quickly braided it. "Maybe I don't like him so well after all."

Lora tied off her braid. "So I take it Louis and Peter were not invited?" When Catty shook her head, Lora linked arms with her and led her out of the dormitory. "Do you suppose he takes all of his girls to balls at the palace?"

"I think Queen Matilda would have something to say about that, don't you?" Catty's smile had returned. She looked down at her feet just as they arrived at the dining hall. "So, do you think he might like me?"

"Maybe," Lora admitted. "I have to say though that I might have had a better idea if you hadn't pushed me into staring at Peter waiting for something that would never happen. I haven't noticed anything except a total lack of his looking at me. I really do believe that we're just friends."

Catty's laugh rang out across the courtyard. "Of course you are," she teased. "But I had you thinking. Wondering. It did you some good, I think. Look how quickly you could part with all that juicy gossip about Regan."

Lora rolled her eyes. "Talking and doing are two very different things," she said as she took Louis' arm. She was very careful to not only walk with Peter. If he did like her, and it was now sounding like he didn't, she didn't want him getting the wrong idea.

They were inside and well into their meal when Catty spoke again. "He's a good kisser."

The fork made a horrible clatter as it hit Lora's plate after she dropped it. "I don't know why I'm surprised," she said.

Catty shrugged. "I'm going to make him wait for more though. My cousin said that's how you snare a husband. You make him believe you're his while never going too far. Lots of kissing and no risk. Win, win." She paused and giggled. "Win, win, and another win. I'd forgotten that I'd be queen."

Lora pushed her dinner around her plate. She envied Catty. Her father was the baron of a minor, but prosperous holding. She was well-connected, and she was a promising swordsplayer. She was pretty. She could kiss or pine after nearly anyone she wanted. It was easy for her to throw caution to the wind and dream about boys.

On the other hand, Lora was common. She had no connections, save for the friendships she made at school and her tenuous arrangement with Lord Allistair. Her father, while a respectable tradesman in Haven Dale, had little money in comparison to the even the lowest members of the gentry. Lora's mousy brown hair, freckles, plain features, and absence of womanly curves made overlooking her lack of fortune difficult. While she was a swordwielder, it remained to be seen if this increased her standing as much any everyone seemed to think it would. Any young man she allowed herself to like just set her up for tears and anguish. No patriarch of any noble family would see even a younger son wed to a peasant. Any kisses she shared made her vulnerable situation even more delicate. If her reputation were marred, any chance she might have had of making a match would be shattered. It would be a stretch for a younger son of a minor branch of a minor house to look at her based on the way being a swordwielder supposedly raised her status.

It is best not to think of kisses, she told herself. But that would be difficult with Catty as her friend. Genea appeared to be fairly reserved. Or she was really good at keeping her exploits to herself. Catty, on the other hand, rarely did anything quietly. Lora did not look forward to what that meant for her future with young men.

CHAPTER 20

Lora found the midwinter holidays more cheerful and lonelier at the same time. Having Catty around made it difficult to study as she was used to. Her friend got bored quickly and was always looking to go to the tailor or milliner or haberdasher or confectioner. Lora was not keen on shopping, as her funds were so limited, and merely tagged along on these excursions. At other times, she was eager to visit with friends. They spent a great deal of time with Genea and Regan as well as a couple of other Academy students who lived in Glimmen. Very little time was spent on schoolwork. That made her nervous about how she would fare when classes resumed.

On a day that Lora was able to escape yet another visit to the milliner, she found herself in the library staring out the window with a diplomacy text open and forgotten in front of her. She sensed someone slide into the seat across from her and started when she realized who it was.

"So, my dear," Lord Cedric said. "I haven't seen you about. I've missed our conversations. Such fresh views you have. It's good for these old bones to hear something new for a change." He ran his hand over his balding pate. The white hairs adorning it on the top were few and far between. "I noticed that Miss Catherine is here for the holidays. You two are quite thick."

"Yes, sir," Lora told him. "It's been nice to have a friend around."

"Indeed," he said. "Your... cousin does not bring you home during the holidays. Do you miss your family?"

Lora was not quite sure what to say. "Of course, I do," she said after a moment. "I saw my father and brother every day until I came here. Now it's been over two years. I'm not sure I'd recognize them. Or if they'd recognize me."

"They would," he assured her. He cleared his throat. "Tell me. Were you close to Lord Allistair or Lady Tiana when you lived in the village? I know you've seen her a bit. That must be reassuring."

"It is." Lora was not sure where the conversation was going. It made her a little bit nervous.

"And they are paying your way while you are here?" Lord Cedric leaned back in his chair and stroked his beard.

"Yes…"

He pursed his lips and hmmph'ed. "That's very kind of them." He stood up and brushed off his tunic. "Well, I won't keep you. I know you're used to studying, and that Miss Catherine has made it difficult to keep up this winter. I wish you a pleasant afternoon." He smiled, picked up his cane, and hobbled off.

Lora stared after him. She wondered if this was his way of reminding her about their conversations or if it was a remark on her choice of friends. Whatever it was, it was odd. She hoped their conversations would stick to theory in the future.

"You'll never guess what," Catty flounced into the chair Lord Cedric had just vacated. She crossed her arms in front of her chest and pouted.

Lora placed her hand over her heart and took a deep breath. She was tired of being startled. "You're right," she admitted. "I won't."

Catty leaned back and placed the back of her hand on her forehead in true dramatic fashion. "Regan invited Peter and Louis to the ball. They can't come, of course, since they've both gone home. But do you see what this means?" Lora did not, so she gestured for Catty to continue. "It means that my kisses mean nothing to him. I'm not any different from any other girl."

"I'm... sorry?" Lora was puzzled. "You don't seem upset. I'm not sure what to say to you."

"I'm not upset," Catty said. "It's very strange." She shrugged. "So would you like to see the new hat I bought?"

Lora sighed and nodded. There was no getting out of oohing and ah-ing over Catty's latest acquisition. It was a garish yellow monstrosity that would have paired nicely with the rancid egg yolk.

She almost wished she had gone with to prevent her friend from making such a ghastly purchase.

CHAPTER 21

The midwinter ball was traditionally held at the palace on midwinter's day. Catty was up at sunrise and decided to wake Lora up as well. Her dress had been hung up for two days to air it out. It was new, and it had been acquired on one of their many trips to the tailor's. Catty had been fitted and refitted so many times it made Lora's head spin. The dress had seemed fine the first time she put it on.

"It's too early," Lora chided. "The ball will just be getting over at this time tomorrow. You'll never make it. You should go back to sleep. Or take a long nap this afternoon. The ball doesn't even start until dinner."

"I know, but I just can't calm down!" Catty grinned and threw a robe over her nightgown. "Genea is lending me her ladies' maid so I can have my hair done up properly. She won't be here for hours and hours. I just don't know how I'm going to pass the day."

Lora rolled her eyes. "We could spar, work on weapons, go riding, anything you want. I could even gag you with some air, if I can manage to grab hold of it. I'd even be willing to sit and embroider if you just need busy hands while you talk."

Catty groaned. "I can't concentrate to do any of those things. And what if I bruised myself—or worse—doing those activities? I wouldn't be able to show my face!"

"Well then let's go get some breakfast."

"No can do. I couldn't eat a bite. Plus I need to be able to draw my laces. That gown is tight enough as it is without throwing griddle cakes and bacon into the equation."

"You have to eat something, Catty. You'll pass out if you don't." Lora swore under her breath and shook her head.

Catty laughed. "Language! What if Mistress Tabitha hears you?"

Lora sighed. She was never going to live down the escapade of breaking her arm. She was still thinking of a response when she realized Catty had begun speaking again. There just would be no calming her down. She shimmied out of her nightgown, threw on her tunic, pants, and a sweater, and went to the dining hall. She ate a quick breakfast and snagged a scone to take back to her friend. When she returned to the dormitory, Catty was asleep.

She shook her head, grabbed her warm cloak, as it was colder outside than she'd anticipated, and headed to the armory. She'd been neglecting her weapons training, and she knew her muscles were going to let her know it. She nodded to Blaine when she got there, went to examine the swords, and stopped when he grabbed her arm.

"You favor that sword too much, lass," he said. "I know you're small, but try the mace. You look like you need to give that wooden post a good beating. It's never as satisfying with a sword."

Lora hated the mace. Blaine knew this and pestered her about it unmercifully. But even though she rolled her eyes, she respected his opinion and bypassed the swords. Once she had indeed given the post a good walloping, she was glad she had chosen that weapon. When she returned it, he winked at her again and told her to come the next day ready to throw some stars. He knew she hated throwing stars too.

She ran to the dorms and then the communal baths as quickly as she could. The wind was merciless to a sweaty body in the winter. Even though she was reasonably fast, she was still cold when she stepped into the water. It warmed her immediately. She had not enjoyed a bath to herself for the entire holiday. She enjoyed the heat soaking into her bones in the quiet. She was sad to get out, but her fingers and toes were shriveled up to practically nothing.

Catty was awake when she returned to the dorms. The older girl had resumed her pacing and was muttering under her breath. Lora was glad she couldn't hear what her friend was saying.

Lora rubbed her hair with her towel, combed it, and rubbed it again. It took forever to dry in the winter, as did most of the other girls' hair, but it was a necessary evil with all of the physical exercise and sweating they did. She donned a dark grey day dress when she was finished and stared at Catty as she paced. Catty was nibbling the now-dry breakfast pastry Lora had brought her hours before.

"This came for you while you were gone," she said as she thrust a small parcel at Lora mid-pace.

The only parcels that ever came for Lora were her clothes and that was only twice a year. This box was far too small. There was a note attached. Catty snatched it up just as Lora had finished reading it.

Catty's mouth formed a perfect O. "I'd forgotten. I'm so sorry. I was so preoccupied with the ball. You must think I'm a terrible friend to forget your birthday."

Lora waved her off as she tried to think of all of her friends' handwriting. The note, which simply wished her a happy birthday, was unsigned and written in block print. She frowned and worked at the knot. Her friends all knew that gifts were forbidden, since she could not reciprocate. She did not like this at all.

Rolling her eyes at her friend's attempts, Catty tore the box away from Lora and undid the knot in half a moment. She was kind enough to give it back to Lora, who just shook her head, unwrapped the paper from around it, and opened it. Her frown deepened as she saw what was inside.

"Ooh! A necklace!" Catty exclaimed. "What a lucky girl! And you said you didn't have any admirers."

Lora did not, in fact, have any admirers. That she knew of. She took the necklace out of the box and tried to appreciate it. It was a dark green stone cut into an oval and polished. It was attached to a black silk ribbon by a plain metal ring. It was very pretty and far too fancy for anything Lora owned. "You should wear it tonight," Lora said as she handed it to Catty. "Your dress is green. It'll go nicely."

Catty shook her head. "As much as I'd like to, I can't Lora. It's your birthday gift from someone and you haven't even worn it yet. What if that someone is at the ball? They'll think you don't like it. So you'll just have to save it until you have occasion to wear it." She paused. "Regan will invite you to the ball next year. You'll be sixteen. Barely. You can wear it then. Now," she placed her hands on her hips for emphasis. "I need your help getting into my corset and dress. That dratted maid of Genea's isn't here yet and the sun is starting to set."

"This could be a mistake," Lora told her as Catty undressed. "You know I'm no good at doing hair."

Catty pursed her lips. She hurriedly put on her underthings and petticoats. "If all else fails, I'll wear it down. I really shouldn't be wearing it up anyway." She fastened her corset on and walked to the timber in the middle of the room that helped hold the roof up. She grasped it and closed her eyes. "I'm ready. Do your worst."

Lora bit her lip. Common women did not wear corsets, and students did not wear them at the Academy. At least, those under sixteen did not wear them. They were considered an impractical frivolity for those training in warcraft. She had seen them being tightened, but had never done it herself. It was not something her two sevendays of lessons from Lady Tiana on how to be a lady included. "I've never done this," she finally admitted.

"Just pull the laces as tight as you can and tie them," Catty laughed. "I keep forgetting you have no older sisters. Didn't your mother wear one?"

"She passed when I was five." Lora was glad she did not have to admit that her mother had not worn one. She wasn't sure how she would've explained that one away.

"I'm sorry. I keep forgetting."

She shrugged. "It's alright." Lora grasped the corset's ties. "Are you ready?" Catty whimpered and nodded, and Lora pulled.

"Harder. Or else the dress won't fit."

Lora pulled as hard as she could and felt the laces give. "Is that enough? Catty grunted an affirmative, and Lora quickly tied them.

Catty stood straight and put her hands on her stomach and back. "Thank you," she whispered. "Would you get my gown so I can step into it? I couldn't bend to pick it up if I wanted to."

"Will it get better?" Lora gestured to the corset.

"Yes," she replied as she stepped into her dress. It was a mint green with tiny, delicate lace trimmings and seed pearls. It cost more money than Lora wanted to think about. "I feel a little funny showing this much skin," Catty continued as Lora did up the tiny buttons on the back. "It's not halfway as daring as some of the older girls' dresses, but my neck feels so bare. Especially with my arms uncovered from the shoulder down."

Lora shrugged. "I suppose I would feel the same way," she said. She regarded her friend for a moment. "You know, I think those silver hair combs your father got you in James Lake would look nice with this. Better yet, I think I might even be able to put them in your hair properly." When Catty nodded in agreement, Lora pulled her trunk over and stood on it. She began brushing out her friend's nut brown locks and felt a pang of envy at the color. Her hair was a dull, mousey brown color that no one would ever think attractive.

"When are you going to grow?" Catty gestured to the trunk Lora stood upon. "I'm not tall and I feel like a giant because you have to stand on that to be just enough above me to brush my hair."

"I don't think my mother was very tall," Lora said as she positioned the combs in Catty's hair. "This may be it for me. I guess it's a good thing I'm a sword*wielder*. I'd be too scrawny to fight on my own."

Catty spun around once Lora was done with her hair. "I wish we had a mirror. There are many at the palace, but it would be nice to see what I look like before I get there." She looked at Lora for a moment. Her friend was still on top of the trunk. "I suppose you're not that short. There are smaller girls at the palace. Men tend to like that. Smaller women make them feel manlier, I guess."

Lora stared down at her hands. "I wouldn't know. I'm not the one who's been practicing at kissing." She jumped off the trunk, pushed it back over by her bed, and looked up at her friend. "My size might make someone feel manlier, but I'm plain, poor, and I have no curves." Catty started to protest, but Lora held up her hand. "Arguing is a waste of time. I know my strengths and weaknesses. It's too bad no one wants a penniless, homely, skinny, mathematician who might burn down their home while throwing a knife at them. I'd be great for that."

"Lora, Lora, Lora," Catty shook her head. "I will argue with you later." She picked up an elaborate fur-trimmed cloak that lay on her bed. "Don't wait up." She smiled, turned, and left.

Seeing as how it was dinner time, Lora grabbed her cloak and headed to the dining hall. She hated discussions of boys and clothes and marriage and kissing. Allowing herself to like someone was just setting herself up for despair. Lady Tiana liked to remind her of that on every visit.

She saw a group of young men near the entrance to the dining hall. There weren't many visitors to the Academy, especially in winter, so she slowed down to get a better look at them. One of them turned to the side, Lora's heart leapt, and she ran toward him. She knew those auburn curls anywhere and a smile touched her lips as she grabbed him in a big hug.

"Whoa there!" the young man stiffened and pushed her off of him. He held her at arm's length and took her measure.

Lora's face was crimson. "I'm so sorry," she sputtered. She had been so sure it had been her friend. "I thought you were someone else. Forgive me." She tried to run past him, but he caught her arm.

"Thought I was someone else?" He raised his eyebrow in surprise. "You must've thought I was Dain then." The young man chuckled. "I should've guessed you were one of his playthings."

The crimson in her face burned brighter. "I'm no one's plaything!" Lora was indignant. "I—I am Lorana of Haven Dale. Dain is my friend."

The young man chuckled. "My mistake," he murmured. "I have heard of you though. You're the other swordwielder. Lora, my brother called you, I think."

"Brother?"

Dain's brother nodded. "I am Phillip of Mount Rathbone. Dain is my younger brother." He cleared his throat. "We look quite alike we're often told."

Lora nodded. "You do," she admitted. "I'm sorry to have troubled you. Please give him my regards." She bobbed a small curtsy and was stopped short by the feel of his hand, still on her arm.

"Dain said you were thirteen."

"That was two years ago, Master Phillip," she said as she ripped her arm from his grasp. Lora did not like the way he was looking at her. She picked up her skirts and ran the few remaining steps inside. She heard their laughter echoing all the way on the far side of the building and she felt her cheeks burning again as she slid into a seat.

Platters of food were brought from the kitchens and placed onto the tables. The food was fancier, by far, than any day of the year. Midwinter feasts brought some students back to the Academy if they were assigned to posts nearby. It was the closest thing to family that many had on this day of thanks.

Lora stared at the food in front of her. She felt strange after her encounter with Dain's brother, and she didn't like it. She did not even move when someone sat beside her.

"It's not like you to hold back at dinner, young miss," Lord Cedric told her as he put a few choice items on her plate. "Missing your friend at the ball, are you?"

Her eyes drifted to where Phillip and his friends had settled. Phillip caught her looking and raised his glass to her. She shuddered and looked back at her plate. "Yes, that's right," she said softly. She felt herself lift her hand and bring her fingers to her mouth. It had been ages since she'd bitten her nails, but she began to do it anyway.

"You can't fool me, Lora," he said. His voice held a sternness she rarely heard. "I take it the young Master Rathbone and his friends caught you unawares? Did you think he was Dain, then?"

Lora nodded. "I did," she replied. "I... don't care for him." Her voice was heavily laced with contempt.

Lord Cedric frowned. "He's usually quite popular with the young ladies, but I can see how he might not run to everyone's tastes," he told her as he pushed her plate closer. "Eat." When Lora picked up her fork and knife and began to dig in, he continued, "Your manners aren't quite the same as other young ladies here, and I think some will take that to mean a certain... Well, they may try to take advantage believing you are encouraging them, even when you are not. That is their reputation, even though it is not yours."

"I understand."

"I don't think they are quite your type. You tend to keep to your small group of friends. Shy, you are," he continued. "If you'd like, I can arrange for one of your teachers to walk you back to your dormitory. Or I can do it, if you are uncomfortable leaving here alone."

"I'll think on it, Lord Cedric," she told him. "I had thought to go to the library before retiring, but I think I will just go to sleep after I'm done eating here." She smiled at him. "Don't worry about me. I'm a swordwielder. Blade and flame at my fingertips and all that."

"Of course you are," he said as he stood. He patted her on the head and walked toward Lord Michael.

The food was good. Ham with cloves and apples. Roast duck with orange and fig and sage stuffing roasted inside. Whipped potatoes. Crusty bread and butter. Pickled beets and sour cream. And apple pie with whipped cream. Lora ate more than her fill even in spite of her stomach being turned by the night's earlier events. This was also the only event at the Academy where wine was served. She hadn't tried it in years past, but had a glass with dinner. She didn't care for the taste and didn't think she would be trying it again anytime soon.

Lora stood up and got a bit dizzy. She shook the cobwebs out of her head and walked toward the door, grabbing her cloak along the way. It had begun to snow sometime during dinner and she trudged through the light dusting, not looking where she was going. She stepped into the girls' dorms for swordsplayers and slammed the door behind her. She collapsed on her bed shortly thereafter.

She awoke in the morning with a dry mouth and a slight headache. She was a little confused as to why she was still in her clothes and boots, but Lora just shrugged it off to the excitement of the day before. She noticed Catty was not in her bed and frowned. It was early to be sure. The sun wasn't fully above the horizon, but she had thought her friend would return some time in the night.

Before she could get off her bed, the door slammed open. Catty's face was chapped and her hands were red from the cold. "The door wouldn't open," she said. "I've been trying to open it for I don't know how long. It wasn't even stuck. It just… didn't move. I finally found Lord Michael, and he cast some kind of wield over it and it opened. I wonder if it froze shut in the night?"

Lora vaguely recalled Lord Cedric walking toward Lord Michael after they had discussed her worries over Phillip. Could they have been worried enough about her to bind the door closed? Surely Phillip wouldn't have followed her in here? He couldn't have thought her hug meant that she was really a loose woman, could he? She tucked her knees into her chest and put her head on them. "I don't think so," she said. "How was the ball?"

Catty's face lit up. "It was amazing!" She twirled and sashayed and fell onto her bed. "I'm ruined for regular life forever. Why can't every day be a ball?"

"So, a good time then? Did you dance with Regan?"

"Yes, I danced with him," she replied. "I danced with him, his friend Geoffrey, Dain, his brother Phillip, Lord Harr—"

"Dain was there?" Lora was hurt that Dain couldn't be bothered to visit even though his brother obviously had made the time.

Catty nodded, missing the way her friend's face fell at the news. "We danced a few times," she said. "I drank too much sparkling white wine and fell down when Regan tried to kiss me—"

"Catty..." Lora chided.

"I know, I know," she groaned. "But it was my first ball, and I was determined to live it up! I guess this is why girls can't be out until they're sixteen. We're too reckless. Oh well."

Lora took a deep breath. "I'm glad you had fun," she said. "I um, I met Dain's brother last night. I thought he was Dain and I ran up to him... Well, I think he thought I was the type of girl, you know... The type of girl who..." She took another deep breath. "He kept watching me. Lord Cedric noticed and I think he told Lord Michael. I think that's what happened to the door. You don't suppose he really would've followed me in here?"

Catty stared at Lora. "He might've," she admitted. "I guess we both could do with a little extra etiquette and decorum in our lives. No more public displays of affection then?" Lora nodded and hid her face in her knees. "Would you really have run up to Dain and thrown your arms around him?"

"That's what I thought I was doing." Lora's voice was muffled. "I was so excited to see him. It's been a while since I've had even a letter from him and I miss him. I didn't even think about what I was doing. I would've done the same to my father or brother." She turned back to her friend. "You didn't kiss anyone but Regan, did you?"

"No," Catty replied. "And I don't think anyone saw us, but still. I'm not a child anymore, and I have to start thinking about my reputation."

Lora was about to reply when the door slammed open. Dain looked furious. His brown eyes were dark with anger and snowflakes were melting in his curly auburn hair. "Are you alright?" he asked.

"You're not supposed to be in here," was all Lora could say.

He strode over to her while she stood up. Dain leaned over her while she cowered down, terrified of her normally jovial friend. "I don't care," he growled. "Did Phillip—Did Phillip—" He shook his head. "He said he met you, Lora. He said... Are you alright?"

"I'm fine Dain," Lora tried to assure him. She looked over at Catty, who was trying to make herself disappear in one of the corners of the room. "Come to the common area and sit. We can talk there."

"I don't want to sit." Dain ran his hand through his hair. It was obvious he hadn't slept. "I just... Was I right to have punched my brother in the face? Should I have drowned him instead? Flayed the skin off his back?" He turned away from her and glanced at Catty who ran toward the bathing area and disappeared.

Lora crossed her arms in front of her chest. "I don't know what you're talking about Dain. Yes, I met your brother. The circumstances were a little unusual. I did not like him at all. We parted ways and that was the end of it. Why are you so upset?"

Dain let out his breath and sank onto another girl's bed. He eyed her as if seeing her for the first time. "No matter what's happened to you over the past two years, you're a child. I'm no saint, but my brother is shameless." He took a deep breath. "He said he tumbled you in the stables. He said he obviously wasn't the first. I know I shouldn't have believed that of you, but you don't know him, Lora. You're like my little sister…"

She swallowed. "That's very kind of you, Dain. I mistook him for you and in doing so, I acted a little foolishly. I caught him in a big hug. I know I shouldn't have done that even with you, but I think he took it the wrong way. I got away from him—"

"Did he hurt you?"

"No," she replied. "He just grabbed my arm and accused me of being your plaything." Lora blushed. "Lord Cedric noticed I was uncomfortable in the dining hall, and I think he told Lord Michael. Catty couldn't open the door until she spoke with him."

"I doubt my brother would stoop so low as that," Dain said after a moment. "Lora, I am sorry. Phillip can be quite charming, as I'm sure you've heard. But he also, well... So you've heard." He stood up and started toward the door. "I'll leave you to yourself. I'm sure you have things to do. Please forgive me for telling Regan what my brother said—"

"Dain, why?" Lora caught her fingers in her braid as she tried to run her fingers through her hair. "Does everyone know?"

He shook his head. "I only told him in case I needed his help to get Phillip to quiet down." Dain looked sheepish. "I'll see you later. I'll be here for a few days before I head back to James Lake with Lord Brandon and his son, Geoff." He gave her a small bow and headed out.

Lora and Catty spent the next few days sparring and fighting with Dain and Regan. Fortunately for Lora, Regan was easily placated about Phillip and talk of the unfortunate incident soon ceased. Especially since Lora set Regan's cloak on fire when at first he refused to let it go. She had been startled, not because it happened, but because it was exactly what she wanted to happen.

She and Dain walked to dinner together the last evening he was going to be in Glimmen. "I hope you're right and this is the beginning of me being able to control my wielding," she was saying. "After two and a half years, I think Lord Michael and Lord Robert were beginning to despair of me. The pompous Lord Jeremy gave up on me sometime last year, but this may bring him round. Maybe I'll even start to call on the other elements consistently—"

"Lora," Dain interrupted.

"Yes?"

"I've been wanting to speak with you, but Catty and Regan have always been around," he said. "It's about what happened with Phillip. I know I promised not to talk about it anymore—"

"Then don't." Lora pulled her arm from his and began to walk faster.

Dain sped up. "Please stop and listen to me." She stopped but did not turn around. "Lora, you're almost of age."

"I'm only fifteen."

"You're almost of age," Dain repeated. "You're young. Your social standing is… Well, you're not of the same standing as most of our acquaintance. I hate to point that out, but it's true. And those make you a target." He crossed his arms in front of his chest. "No one takes young girls seriously and without a powerful family to back you up, if anything were to happen, you'd be left alone. Friendless. Possibly raising… Well, you'd be alone. If anyone ever bothers you in the future, please talk to Regan. He thinks of you as I do. He will do everything he can to make sure you're alright. Even if what happens between you and whoever is consensual, if you're left by the wayside, he will help you."

Lora stared ahead toward the dining hall. "You make me sound like a harlot. Or like I will be one once I start finding boys to kiss."

Dain shook his head. "I don't mean to in the slightest, but you know how all the blame is placed on you girls when we young men are almost always the culprits." He walked up to her and held out his arm. When she took it, he let out a breath of air he hadn't realized he'd been holding. "I care about you, Lora. I want the best for you. I know you think you're not good enough, but you're wrong. We all think so." He led her inside and didn't say another word about it.

CHAPTER 22

The next term came quickly, much to Lora's relief. Lora improved on her wielding almost exponentially. Lord Robert asked her if anything had happened to break her block, and she denied it. Lord Michael caught her eye and she just shook her head. He did not bring up the subject. She thanked him for respecting her privacy.

"Miss Lorana," he had said. "You're hardly the first girl we've had to seal that door for, and you won't be the first one that gets talked about."

Lord Jeremy was removed as her independent study teacher, as her skills with multiple elements were beyond his level of expertise. He was a fire and essence wielder, but could not help her with water, earth, or air. Lord Michael could have taught her about wielding all of the elements, as his gifts were the same as hers, but he and Lord Robert both insisted that multiple teachers kept your mind from getting too complacent and unimaginative. Since she liked and respected both of them, she was happy with the change to their supervision.

Sylvane continued to be a menace. People found out about Lora's altercation with Phillip, the princess among them. There were red ribbons, bits of red lace, and a red sash left on Lora's bed by someone, and she could only think it was her that put them there. She made a public display of burning them after each made its appearance, but they just kept coming.

In the spring, Lora sat out on the stoop with Catty while she tried to light candles and snuff them out. She struggled with control and Lord Robert had set her this exercise to do in her spare time. As a result, she had a pile of wax lumps sitting on the bare stone of the courtyard with a large circumferential area around them free of all debris.

"You need some new dresses," Catty told her, her mouth full, of caramel. The result of her recent trip to the confectioner was a large box of the things.

Lora closed one eye and pointed at a candle. It went up in flames and a gust of wind blew the remains a few feet back before it went out. "I'm waiting until after the summer," she said as she pointed to the next candle in line. She caught the wick, but the flame was about six feet high. A gust of air smashed the candle flat.

Catty frowned and swallowed her candy. "You've grown," she pointed out. "You're still short, of course. But I can't have you walking around my father's castle with your ankles showing."

"I can't go to your father's castle," she said, attempting to light the next candle. "Cousin Allistair will stop paying my way here if I leave."

"I told you that he doesn't need to know." Catty eyed a caramel and popped it into her mouth. "My father said he didn't care if you came. Our carriage is coming for me anyway. He's feeding our household anyway. The room you'd be staying in is always there. It's no bother."

Lora shook her head. "What if Cousin Tiana comes and I'm not here? I can't risk that." She pointed and the entire row of candles went up in flames. Her eyes widened and a gust of air came down so strong that it knocked both of them over.

Pursing her lips, Catty sat back up and regarded her friend. "You still need new clothes. You're popping out of your bodice, if you couldn't tell." She crossed her arms in front of her chest. "Why give her highness another thing to criticize?"

"Nobody cares but her."

"That's not true," Catty said. She tsk'ed and shook her head. "No one would like it if your seams ripped in the middle of class, especially you."

"Fine. I'll go tomorrow. It's a rest day. I'm sure Mistress Bethany has something ready-made that will serve while the rest are being made."

"You're not seriously going to wear the same dress every day while you're waiting for your new clothes, are you? You'd be better off getting some sort of sweater, just in case." Catty nodded. "Mistress Bethany will know what you need. Oh, and since we'll have our own rooms in the fall—all fourth years and above do, you know—

we can have our evening gowns with us. So, you'll be needing corsets

as well. We'll wear them to dinner as practice."

Lora rolled her eyes. "I'm not sure what you think we're going

to do with multiple evening gowns and corsets," she said. "You may

be sixteen now, but I'm not. Even if I was, my social circle is not the

same as yours."

"Lora, Lora, Lora..." Catty raised her eyes to the sky. "Someday

I'm going to tell you just how ridiculous you are, and you're going to

listen. For now, think on this. You're in our social circle. All of ours.

Regan is the prince. He will be king someday. He is your friend. You're

in his circle. Regardless of your birth, financial situation, or looks,

that's where you are. It counts for a lot. There's no arguing with that.

Everything else is gravy."

The rest of the evening was fairly quiet. Lora did not try

lighting any more candles, and Catty did not try to persuade her how

to dress or spend her holidays. The next day was different. Lora was

going to try and see if holding the candle while trying to light it would

help her control. After all, her own powers wouldn't hurt her, would they? Once Catty realized what she meant to do, she grabbed the candles away, chucked the across the room, and dragged her friend away to Mistress Bethany's.

"Tut, tut," Mistress Bethany said as she took in Lora's appearance. "I'd say you're about done growing, Miss Lorana. At least in height. Perhaps I can leave extra seam allowance in the bodices of the dresses I assume I'm to be making. That way you won't need to come back here for new dresses for a while. Just alterations."

"That's very kind of you," Lora told her. Mistress Bethany's assistant was busy taking her measurements, so she was standing very still.

Catty smirked. "You'll want a set of measurements for an evening gown too," she put in.

Mistress Bethany looked up from her list of measurements. "Is that so? I guess you'll be needing a corset too."

"She'll need one for dinner as well as one for her gown," Catty replied for her.

"Three sets of measurements then." Bethany glanced down at her sheet of parchment and nodded. "I'll grab a corset, and we'll get started."

"I can't wait." Catty clasped her hands together and giggled.

Lora was nearly purple with indignation. "I'm standing right here," she said, taking the corset Mistress Bethany handed her. She fastened it as she had seen Catty do and frowned.

Catty led Lora over to some hand grips that had been bolted into the wall for just such a purpose. Lora grabbed them and took a deep breath as she was instructed. She felt Mistress Bethany take her laces and begin to pull. A noise escaped her mouth with her breath. It was a sound of surprise, shock, and discomfort.

"All done," Mistress Bethany said. "Get her measurements so I can get the other corset."

Lora's eyes were practically bulging out of her head. "Catty you lied," she wheezed. "You said it wasn't that bad. You said that you got used to it quickly. I can't wear this." She gasped as she tried to hyperventilate. The dratted thing even denied her of that.

Mistress Bethany returned as her assistant was just finishing up. She unhooked the corset and quickly slipped the other one on. It was snug before the laces were drawn and was even tighter than the other one afterward. It was cut low, and Lora blushed as she saw herself in the mirror. "It's a woman's garment, Miss Lorana," she said. "Your birthday is later in the winter, if memory serves. Hopefully you'll be able to resign yourself to that by then." She looked over to Catty. "I assume I'll be waiting to use these measurements until then, Miss Catherine?"

"Yes, I'm afraid so," Catty told the tailor. "She won't come to Arbor Cove with me this summer or else she'd need a gown sooner. Probably at the start of the winter holiday. I'll bring her by and you can modify them."

"Very good," Mistress Bethany said. She looked thoughtfully at Lora. "I'm sure I can come up with something that your cousin will approve of. Now let us pick out some fabrics and styles. I can't bear to have you wearing that same boring dress style anymore. Three years is long enough."

Lora sighed. Or sighed as much as she could with an evening gown corset on. In the end, she chose a russet, a dark blue, a dark pink, and a muted green for everyday and a slate grayish brown color for dinner. She refused the elaborate styles Mistress Bethany and Catty wanted for her, but she was certain the tailor had ideas of her own about what she would make. Lora figured it was just as well. She took the vest that Catty picked out for in case she busted a seam in her bodice and bid Mistress Bethany farewell.

The parcel containing her new dresses arrived a sevenday later, which Lora expected. Mistress Bethany had shown herself to be extremely consistent over the past few years. The dresses were mostly as they had discussed. Her biggest concern was the fit of her dinner dress.

"It looks fine," Catty told her before they left the dormitory for dinner. "Your chest is not showing. Just your collarbones. It only feels like it's showing because of how the corset emphasizes your curves. Puts them on display, if you will."

"I don't need anything on display." Lora looked down and frowned. She had been walking back and forth for several minutes hoping to get comfortable before they headed to dinner.

Catty crossed her arms in front of her chest. "I was going to save this conversation until we got you ready for your first ball, but I think now is a good time—"

"Save it."

"No, now is a good time," Catty said. "Your actions here at the Academy have raised you far beyond the station of your birth. You may not have money, but you will always have your title. You're a swordwielder and that is more important than most of the so-called important people in Ydris. That alone would make you a match if you want one, which I'm not sure you do. Secondly, you're not the same person you were when you got here. You're confident now, sure of yourself. You walk taller—you *are* taller. You have the body of a woman, and an attractive one at that. You complain about your hair. It's lightened up into a nice golden brown, which has completely changed the shade of your eyes. Yes, you are my friend and I am biased, but you should know me well enough to know that I won't sugar coat things for you."

Lora looked down at her hands and walked toward the door. She opened it, realized that Catty was at her shoulder, and grasped her friend's hand. Coming out like this was a big step, especially after the words of encouragement Catty had foisted upon her. They walked down the two steps leading from the dormitory to the ground. She looked up and caught Genea's eye as she winked at her. The healing wielder had begun wearing a corset to dinner as soon as Catty had and she came over to Lora's other side and took that hand. The boys weren't there yet, but she could see them across the courtyard.

When they got there, Regan immediately offered Lora his arm. When they began walking toward the dining hall, he said, "You'll let me know if anyone bothers you." It was not a question.

"I don't know why they would, but I will if it makes you feel better," she replied.

Regan smiled down at her, his hair flopping down onto his forehead. "It does," he said.

She smiled back and tucked a lock of no-longer mousey brown hair behind her ear. "Something occurred to me, your highness." When he raised an eyebrow at her use of his honorific, she laughed. "Since you're so insistent, is there someone you think might bother me?"

He stared ahead for a moment, lost in thought. "There are a few," Regan admitted. When Lora opened her mouth to protest, he added, "Don't let it go to your head."

CHAPTER 23

Lora pointed at the candle and a small flame flickered at the wick. She smiled, closed her fist and a small ball of water appeared, she opened her hand and it fell on to the candle, smothering the flame. There was a line of candles that had been similarly treated before it. She drew a circle in the air and a ring of earth rose around each candle, and when she flicked her fingers, a breath of wind blew the disturbed earth away.

"Now that you've mastered those child's parlor tricks, would you care to learn to light your sword on fire?" Lord Michael said from behind her.

She stood up and dusted her hands off on her skirts. She'd gone out to the practice yards for her exercises because there was no dirt atop the cobblestones in the courtyard for her to practice with. "I thought you said that flaming swords did little but inspire fear in your opponent."

"I did say that," he replied. "Sometimes that's all you will need. Now go and see Blaine and get a sword." When she turned toward the dormitories Lord Michael said, "That's not the way to the armory."

"Yes, but I can't fight like this," Lora said as she gestured to her dress. She was wearing the pink one and didn't wish to get it any dirtier than it already was.

Lord Michael stared at her. "You will not always fight in pants and a tunic. Or leathers. Or armor. It's time you learned how to fight with those blasted skirts getting tangled about you. Now go get your sword."

Lora bobbed a small curtsy and ran toward the armory. She was flushed and sweaty when she arrived, and Blaine laughed at the sight of her. "Lord Michael's going to put you through the ringer today, lass. He told me as much." He handed her the sword she worked with most often and shooed her away.

She nearly ran and hid, but she knew her punishment would be ten times worse for running away than it would be for standing up and fighting her teacher. She strapped the sword to her hip already not liking the way it tangled in her legs and skirts. Lora did not want to admit that Lord Michael was right, but she knew he was. When she returned to the practice yard, she winced.

"Took you long enough, girl," Lord Robert said from his perch on the fence. "I'm not here to fight you, so don't worry. I'm just here in case you set your pretty head of hair on fire." He grinned and an amorphous shape rose out of a bucket near him.

Lora envied him that he didn't need to gesture to control his elements. She hoped she would attain that level of control someday. She sighed and stepped into the yard. She hung back by the fence, unsure what to do.

"Draw your sword," Lord Michael told her as he drew his. She tentatively drew hers, wary that she was shredding her skirts as she did do. He lowered his sword and stared at her scornfully, "Don't be ridiculous." Her cheeks flamed and she held her sword at ready. "Good," he told her. "Now treat the blade as you have been those candle wicks. It's no different."

She looked at her sword and a ten foot flame arced out from it. Lora nearly dropped it in surprise. She quickly snuffed it out with air, took a breath, and tried again. This time, a lazy flame rolled over the metal's surface.

"Don't let it go out," he said. He grinned and ran at her.

The flame went out, she clumsily thrust an air shield in front of her, which Lord Michael batted away easily. She crouched into a fighting stance, since she really didn't know what else to do. Lora felt her sword being extricated from her hand by hot tendrils of air just as the air was knocked out of her by Lord Michael's body. He twisted her body and slammed her into the fence, bending her over it. She felt his breath on her neck and froze, the point of the exercise becoming clear. She closed her eyes as she heard a dagger being drawn and ground her teeth in frustration. In hand-to-hand combat, like most women, she was lost if she did not have speed on her side. Obviously, that was the case in this instance. But a niggling feeling at the back of her mind reminded her that this exercise was also about swordwielding.

Lora's eyes popped open as she felt the blade on her neck. Her brows furrowed and she heard a shocked exclamation followed by a stream of curses that colored her cheeks. The weight on her back quickly went away, and when she stood up, she saw Lord Michael stalking away, holding his burned hand before him. He was still cursing. She heard clapping and turned to see Lord Robert still watching her.

"You won't catch him by surprise like that again, Miss Lorana," he said as he hopped down off the fence. "Obviously, we need to speak to Master Karl if he isn't teaching you girls to break that hold. It's not difficult to do." He studied her. "In any case, you can see that it's not all about exploding earth and flaming swords. As a woman, it's also about self-protection. We teach all of the wielders to use their various skills in self-defense. It seems we have been neglecting you thinking that your swordsplay teachers were taking care of that."

"Yes, Lord Robert," she said with a shaking voice. Lora went to retrieve her sword and felt a hand on her wrist as she stood.

Lord Robert's eyes had softened. "Are you alright?"

"Yes," she nodded. "I take harder licks than that from Peter."

"Yes, but not like that and never from us," Lord Robert told her. "I know it's your summer holidays, but I've never actually seen you holidaying. Michael and I felt like we should take the opportunity to start really swordwielding in practice, instead of in theory. Since you're a bit behind schedule—" He held up his hands as she frowned. "It's been three years, and I do recall you boasting you'd be here in less than two and a half. So technically, we *are* behind schedule. And you're not as adept in your swordsplay as we'd like. Too much time spent reading and talking with Lord Cedric, I'd wager." He scratched his iron gray hair. "I'm glad you're alright. But if Michael had really intended to harm you, I don't think you'd have come away from that unscathed. You're a young woman—"

"I'm still fifteen," she growled.

Lord Robert rolled his eyes. "Whatever. You're a young woman and anything can happen when you're roaming around Glimmen or skulking around in dark corners." Lora blushed again. He laughed, rustled her hair, bowed at the neck, and walked away.

Lora took a deep breath and half ran to the armory with her sword. She handed it to Blaine, thanked him, and ran off toward their healer's complex. She arrived out of breath to see a still-swearing Lord Michael sitting with a patient healer.

His eyes darkened when he saw her. "You've been holding out on me."

"No I haven't."

"You've learned to heat metal. That's no simple skill, Lora," he said as the healer continued to clean his hand.

Lora bit her lip. "I've never done it before. You scared me," she admitted. "In all of that, it occurred to me what the original point of the lesson was. Fire is the easiest for me, so I did the only thing I could think of."

Lord Michael hmmph'ed. "You, who set people's cloaks on fire with a flick of your wrist. Heating my dagger to the point it could be reworked by a blacksmith was the first thing that came to your mind?" He shook his head and removed his spectacles with his free hand. "Did you speak to Robert?"

"Yes," she nodded. "He said we needed to work on some things."

"We do."

Lora winced at the sternness in his voice. "I'm sorry."

He waved her off with his good hand. "Don't be sorry," he said, gritting his teeth. The healer had begun to knit the tissues of his hand back together. "Work harder. Get better. Now get out."

As Lora walked back to her room, she thought about the fight. She understood that even with all of her training, she could be caught unawares and overcome by a common street thug. It was a sobering thought. She stared at the door to her new, private room and something dawned on her. There was more protection in an open air room shared with twenty other girls than there was behind a private locked door. This lesson was probably no coincidence. She went inside and bound the door with air, even as she locked it.

A quick glance down at her skirts revealed three neat foot-long slices. Her bodice was ripped in front and on one sleeve. The small looking glass told her that her hair was a fright. Lora told herself that she got off easy.

A knock sounded at her door. She released the air and called, "Who is it?"

"It's me."

"You're mad if you think I'm going to open the door for you, Louis," she said. "You're not supposed to be in here."

"I came to see if you were alright," his voice said from behind the door. "Your fight with Lord Michael has spread through the Academy like wildfire. Well, those of us too stupid to have left for the holidays, anyway. He's a formidable opponent. I just wanted to make sure you were all on one piece."

Lora sighed and unbolted her door. She opened it and looked at her friend. "Satisfied," she asked.

Louis winced. "Well, I guess Peter's made you look worse. You do look terrible though."

"I was about to change when you knocked." She crossed her arms in front of her chest and winced.

"See a healer and make sure your ribs aren't broken," he gestured. "Well, I see you're in one piece. I'll leave you to it. I'd offer to help you out of that, but I prefer not to have my hands melted off." He smiled sheepishly.

"I'd love help," she told him. At his shocked expression, she continued, her face alight with a grin, "Please let Mistress Tabitha know on your way out." She shoved him unceremoniously out of her room, slammed, and bolted her door. She slipped the air binding into place and laughed.

The following sevenday, Lora was surprised by a visit from Lady Tiana. Her belly was round with child, and she looked angry and cross.

"What a marvelous surprise, Cousin Tiana," Lora said to her when she saw her. "I'm happy for you and Lord Larence. I'm surprised you would travel in your state though. Come, sit down here." She grasped Lady Tiana's head and led her to a sofa in the dormitory common area.

Lady Tiana arched an eyebrow at her. "Thank you. I will tell him. We are traveling to Haven Dale. I cannot bear the heat of Rock Harbor, so I am hoping it will be cooler there. This child is roasting me from the inside."

"Please give my regards to Cousin Allistair and Lady Frances when you see them," she said. "Now, to what do I owe the lovely surprise of seeing you?"

"It has been some months," Tiana confessed. "I would not have you think you are being neglected." She eyed her critically. "I see it has happened then. Your bosom has grown, so I must think you have started your courses."

Lora ground her teeth together. This seemed to be the only thing Lady Tiana ever wanted to talk to her about. "Yes, Cousin. I have begun wearing corsets to dinner, as well. It is expected now, and I'm told that I will also be invited to the midwinter ball at the palace."

Lady Tiana nodded. "That is kind of them to think of you. You remember what I have told you about relations?"

A few heads turned toward them. Lady Tiana had not bothered to lower her voice. Lora was thankful that there were not many people around them. She figured it must be due to her pregnancy that the normally very proper woman would speak so in company. "Yes, I do," she coughed.

"And?"

"And nothing," Lora told her in a low voice. "I heed your advice. In truth, no one has sought me out, but if they had they would not have found me willing. We also have been taught self-defense, should we ever be accosted."

"Good," she said. Her face turned thoughtful. "My brother thinks we should increase your allowance. He thinks two silvers a month is stingy. I imagine your friends here have more." She sighed. "He has thought to increase it to five silvers per month."

Lora calculated in her head that she would have in two months what it had taken her all year to save previously. "That is very generous," she said. "I thank you."

"Your father has been asking after you," she said absently as she fanned herself with her hand. "What shall I tell him when I see him?"

"Well, you may tell him that I love him and miss him greatly." Lora was startled by the question. Lady Tiana never brought up her family. "That I am doing well in my studies. You may convey my regards to my brother, as well." She was now certain that the pregnancy was affecting her judgment. "Tell them... Tell them I can set my sword on fire and block blows with a shield of air. I think that will give them a very glamourous picture of life here."

Tiana chuckled. "You have come far," she said. "It is... a pleasure to speak with you now. I understand you are friends with the prince?" Lora nodded and Tiana smiled. "I am glad for you, Cousin Lorana." She stood and placed her hand on her belly. "I will leave you now. No doubt you are busy. It has been a pleasure." She took Lora's hands in hers, bobbed a small curtsy, and left.

To say Lora was astonished was an understatement. She stared at the door so long that two people came and left before she began to walk back to her small room. She stopped when a voice called to her. She smiled when she noticed who it was.

"I just ran into your cousin," Regan said. "How wonderful! When does she expect the child?"

"Late in the autumn, I believe," she replied. She gave him a deep curtsy and he scowled. "We never pay you your rightful due, your highness. We do everything else as properly as we can, so..." She shrugged.

Regan rolled his eyes. "I can see your cousin's influence. You're always so stuffy when she comes."

Lora frowned. "Stuffy?"

"You try to impress her when she's here," he explained. "It's like I am with my father. I am what I am because of him. Just as you are what you are because of her and Lord Allistair. But it's not you. I prefer you less formal."

She wanted to tell him that she was not at all what she appeared, but she swallowed that notion as it appeared. "I'm not sure what to say to that, Regan."

"Just that," he said, taking her arm. "Come on. I'm having Louis and you over for dinner."

Lora paled. "I'm not dressed. I have nothing to wear." Her hands grew clammy. She had never been to the palace. She thought she had some time to acclimate herself to the idea of possibly going to the ball during the midwinter holidays. This was horrible.

"I'll give you time to dress, and I am acutely aware that you have several suitable articles of clothing appropriate for dinner," he said, gently removing her arm from his.

She shook her head and stared at the ground.

"It's just Louis and me, Lora," he said. "And maybe my sister. My father won't be there. There won't be anyone you don't know. It'll be like eating dinner here, except with better food. And better service."

"I can't."

"I don't understand you."

"*Prince* Regan," she began, "shall I describe my own home in Haven Dale to you? You'd find it charming, I'm sure." Lora's hands began to shake. "Downstairs is a work area, an open kitchen and eating area, and a space for sitting. It's about the size of this room we're in now." She gestured around the common room, which held three sofas and was cramped. "Upstairs was one large sleeping area. Just before I left, my father had curtained off one corner to give me privacy. I had thought it so grand to have my own space. My room here is larger." She took a deep breath. "Do you understand me now?"

His hands were clenched into fists at his sides. His hair had fallen into his face so that she couldn't see his eyes. "I don't care and nor should you," he grumbled.

Lora raised her eyebrows. "I'd rather not get used to the palace. Or anywhere else like that. I'll be going back home when my training is done. It will be far easier if I imagine those places, rather than experience them."

"And if you are assigned to the palace for training?" he asked as he crossed his arms over his chest. "What then?"

"Why do you always have to be right?" She turned away and took a deep breath.

"Because I will be king someday," he said. His voice was quiet. Lora knew he was acutely aware that he had hurt her feelings. "And I can almost guarantee that you won't be going back to your father's house." He shook his head. "Enough of this. I'll have Mistress Tabitha come help you dress." He turned and left.

Lora walked quickly back to her room. Regan was her friend, and as much as she knew he had not wanted to hurt her feelings, she also knew he would not want her to dwell on making him angry. Both feelings would pass soon enough, but it was hard. She blinked back a few tears when she got to her room, opened her wardrobe, and looked inside. She now had two dresses for dinner. The dark grey one was heavy and less suited for summer. She had not yet worn her other dress, as it verged on the point of being too fancy for the Academy. Mistress Bethany had done some pretty fast talking in order to get her to agree to it. It was a coppery gold, the color of sunset. The material was silky and soft and it was tastefully trimmed with ribbons.

A moment later, Lora let Mistress Tabitha into her room. The older woman noticed how distraught she was and pulled her into a hug. "He can be a bit of a boor," she said. "It's a failing of all noblemen. Is this what you'll be wearing? It's lovely. It will make your hair positively glow. Will you be wearing it up?"

Lora blinked. "No," she stammered. "Not until midwinter."

Mistress Tabitha smiled. "Of course, I apologize. All of you young girls seem to be growing up so quickly." She gestured for Lora to step out of her gown.

Lora quickly complied and got into her corset. She held onto her bedpost as Mistress Tabitha drew her laces. Even though she hated it, she found she was getting used to it, and even felt a little odd to eat dinner without it. She found herself wearing it even if she dined alone. She stepped into her dress and Mistress Tabitha fastened the back. "Thank you for helping me," she said. "You know you don't have to."

"Not at all," she said. "I know your friends have gone for the summer and you've no ladies maid. It's nothing." Mistress Tabitha smiled. "I miss having my daughter around and you remind me of her. She married just before you started here."

"Thank you again," Lora said. The two women walked to the common area together, where they found Louis and Regan.

Louis' face broke into a grin. "What have you done with our Lora?" He laughed and shook his head. He held out his arm. "You'll raise my stock a hundred fold. I'll have to insist you walk with me everywhere now."

Lora blushed. "What an odd compliment," she said, wishing she could punch him in the arm. She stared for a moment and did it anyway.

"Ow!"

"Shall we?" She grabbed Louis' arm before he could pull it away. "Regan?"

Regan nodded. "I apologize, but there will be a couple of more at dinner. I'm sure you'll approve. Dain is in town. Lord Brandon has come to talk to my father about some inquiry or other of the Korlisseans. So Dain and Geoff are with him, of course."

"Geoff?" she asked as they walked outside.

"You've not met Geoff?"

Louis guffawed when Lora shook her head. "Lucky girl."

Regan climbed into his carriage and held his hand out for Lora. "I've known him forever, his father being my father's chief advisor and all. He can be a little arrogant—"

"A little?" Louis let go of Lora's hand as she stepped into the carriage.

"A lot then," Regan grumbled. "He's a good sort though."

Regan and Louis teased Lora about her enthusiasm for the city as they drove through it. "You forget that I walk from the Academy to a few shops and that I've driven in once from home when I was twelve. This is all new to me. I am sure that you two are much the same whenever you go somewhere you've never been."

"I feel sorry for whoever you travel with to your first assignment," Louis chuckled. "It'll take three times as long to get there for all of your stopping and looking."

Lora stuck her tongue out at him. She did not care that it was improper. "I hope I get stuck with you then," she retorted.

They bickered back and forth for the rest of the short ride, and Lora got more and more nervous. The palace came into view and her palms started to sweat. She didn't realize she was holding her breath until spots swam in front of her eyes. Regan shook her arm as she started to faint. Before he could admonish her, she said, "It wouldn't have happened if your damned house wasn't so big, your highness."

"You can't help where you're born, Miss Lorana," Regan said as he punched Louis, whose chuckles had deteriorated into a wheezing kind of guffaw, in the arm. "Anyway, we're here. Try to breathe as we walk through the hallway. The route through the hallways is ten times as long as the length of the outside of the building." They descended from the carriage when it stopped, and he offered her his arm.

Lora stared straight ahead as they walked through the palace. She knew that if she looked around at the rich, beautiful surroundings that she would feel even worse. The multitude of servants who bowed at the prince as they walked by had her squeezing her eyes shut as well. She started to hyperventilate until Regan elbowed her

"You know me," he murmured, pushing his blond hair out of his eyes with his free hand. "Just think of it like the Academy. It's a big place with lots of people living and working there, and there's one important guy in charge of it all. My father, instead of Lord Everett. You feel normal when you're there, right? You should feel fine when you're here." He pulled her in closer.

When they arrived at the Blue Dining Room, as it was called, Lora's nervousness faded. Dain stood there laughing with a young man who could only be Geoffrey of James Lake. Sylvane stood with them, her arms across her chest, glaring. When they were noticed, Sylvane frowned.

"Hello, Ready-Made," Sylvane called. "Lovely of you to join us."

"Cut it out, Sylvane," Regan shot back. "Everyone here is a welcome guest. I see you everyday, so your absence is no great loss to our party." Sylvane pouted prettily, but did not reply. He nodded toward Dain and the young man he was speaking with. "Geoff! You've heard us talk about Lora often enough, haven't you?" He walked her over to where they stood. "I could've sworn you two had met. Miss Lorana of Haven Dale meet Master Geoffrey of James Lake."

Lora curtsied when Regan let go of her arm. "Please to meet you, Master Geoffrey," she told him.

"The pleasure is all mine," he said as he rose from an elegant bow. Geoffrey took her hand and kissed the back of it. "And please call me Geoff. It'd be odd for you to call me anything else with these fools around."

She blushed. No one had ever kissed her hand before. "Please call me Lora. No one calls me Lorana but my cousins and our teachers."

Geoffrey held out his arm for her. When Lora took it, he led her to a place at the table. "Of course, Lora. Here, sit by me. I know everyone else here, and I fear we've exhausted all topics of conversation, so it will be a nice change to speak with someone new." He let go of her, smiled, and ran his hand through his blond waves, as if to fluff them up a bit.

Lora's gaze slid from Geoffrey to Dain, who was making a gagging gesture, and then to Regan. The prince was trying very hard not to laugh. Louis was busy distracting Sylvane and hadn't seen the interchange. She felt her face redden. It was very uncomfortable to be under so many different types of scrutiny.

At that moment, a servant appeared and rang a small silver bell. "My lords and ladies," his voice rang out. "Dinner is served."

The group gathered around the table. The young ladies sat, quickly followed by the young men. Six servants then appeared, each carrying a plate topped with a silver cloche. As one, they placed them in front of the diners and removed the cloches.

Lora stared at her plate. She had no idea what was on it and could not fathom how to eat it. She made eye contact with Dain, who sat across from her. He smiled, picked up the morsel with his hand and took a small bite. "I just love smoked oysters on melba, don't you?" he asked.

"Obviously," she told him, mirroring his actions. The oysters were cold and bitter in her mouth. Her muscles seized. She wanted nothing more than to spit the offending morsel out, but was forced to chew and swallow. She placed the oyster back onto her plate, dabbed her mouth with her napkin, and reached for her glass of wine. Table manners had been discussed back at the beginning of her first year. They were hard to practice because of the way meals were served and the type of food that was served at the Academy. Seeing as how this meal started with a cold hors d'oeuvres, Lora reached back into the recesses of her mind for traditional seven course meal menus to try and anticipate which forks and knives to use.

Dain smiled and tipped his head toward Geoffrey, who evidently was regaling Lora with some tale of a buck he had gotten on a hunt. Her eyes narrowed at her friend. His smile grew. "Tell me, Lora," he interjected when Geoffrey was taking a breath. "How have your holidays been?"

"I melted a knife to Lord Michael's hand," she said nonchalantly.

"I've always been jealous of your fire," he replied. "Was it the first time he let you swordwield?"

Lora nodded, trying very hard not to grin at Geoffrey's obvious discomfiture at the thought of her using a sword and shooting flames out of her hands. "He'd disarmed me, and I did it on instinct."

Regan frowned. "He cracked your rib, if I recall."

"Very few young men at James Lake learn swordsplay at the Academy," Geoff put in. "None of the ladies do. I'd be very distraught if my sister had been handled in such a way."

Their cold appetizers were then removed by one set of servants. Another set revealed small bowls of soup. Lora picked up a spoon and checked her choice with Dain. He nodded and she began eating. "It was not my plan to learn swordsplay when I arrived in Glimmen. I was here to learn wielding, to keep from burning down my village, if nothing else. The sword part was a surprise."

"Haven Dale must be very backward indeed," Sylvane said quietly. "Your manners are coarse now, but you were a barbarian when you arrived." She was seated on the other side of Geoffrey. "The first time I met Lorana here, was at dinner. It's self-serve from large platters in the middle of the table. Well, she grabbed a meat pie with her hand and just started eating it. No utensils. It was quite shocking."

Lora smiled. "Haven Dale is small, but it's not the town that's at fault," she said as she lifted her spoon from her bowl. The soup was green with white specks and tasted of broccoli and goat cheese. She looked at Geoffrey while her bite of soup cooled. "We are far removed from my cousin, Lord Allistair, if you catch my meaning."

"You don't speak much of your family," Louis said. "You never go home, and they never visit. Just Lady Tiana on occasion."

This was dangerous ground and Lora wished to change the subject. "There are no means for visits," she explained. "It's just my father and older brother, Shawn. They never change. Although, I understand Shawn is courting some girl or other." She shrugged and took her bite, careful not to slurp.

That seemed to satisfy Louis, and he went back to his soup. Dain winked at her, which made her blush. Regan merely looked thoughtful.

The fish course followed, which was some sort of sole in a creamy sauce and an unidentifiable vegetable. Dain kindly worked the name of what they were eating into their conversations whenever he could. Regan seemed to catch on to what they were doing and was quick to name the palate cleanser a bitter orange sorbet. The taste stuck on her tongue, and Lora did not really find her palate much cleansed.

"Ah, veal!" Geoffrey exclaimed when the meat course was brought forth. "We keep veal calves at James Lake."

Lora was tired of hearing about James Lake. It seemed that they had everything there. She found it boring that everything possible could be found or occur there. She didn't need to ask any questions about it, since it had everything. She only had to assume. "Fascinating," she finally offered.

Regan choked on his wine and tried to hide his laughter in a cough. "James Lake is a nice place," he said after he recovered. "The weather is quite fine. The lake is picturesque, and you can see the mountains in the distance. I spent a good deal of time there as a boy. Geoff and I made quite the pair in those days."

"I like to think we still do, Regan," Geoffrey said. His hazel eyes were quite earnest.

A salad of kale and tomato followed. If nothing else, the meal made Lora acutely aware of what foods she did not need to try again. And perhaps how to eat food she didn't like without letting on that she didn't like it. She was starting to change her mind about wine though. It was no surprise that the palace would have better vintages than the Academy.

"How long are you here?" she asked Dain, finally finding an opportunity to speak with him while Geoffrey was occupied with Sylvane.

Dain shrugged. "Lord Brandon is here to bring a missive to the king from King Shane of Korlisse. It's the same every summer. This for that. It's worked for the past few years. No one's been especially offended in a while, which is nice. While I'm prepared for it, I'm not interested in going to war."

"Lord Cedric says relations are better than they have been for as long as he can remember," she said. "In spite of that, I hope you will be able to stay awhile. I'm sure Lord Michael or Lord Robert would be thrilled to give you a trouncing."

"That's a very interesting way to try and entice me to stay," Dain teased. "Reminding me of what violence my teachers can do to me."

"Violence?" Geoffrey asked. "Good heavens. Perhaps I should convince my father to leave sooner. We'd planned on staying a few sevendays, but I'm sure he'd prefer you in one piece."

Dessert was served. Lora smiled. It was a mess of caramel and chocolate and summer-ripe berries on top of a shortbread. She was glad to finally have something her stomach could count on to be edible. "It's good for Dain to keep in practice. Our teachers wouldn't do him any lasting damage. And any temporary injuries would be healed up by the wielders."

"You don't heal?" Geoffrey pushed his dessert around his plate.

Lora shook her head. "I use fire, water, earth, and air. I also use my essence, but we're not quite sure what aspect of it though. Probably distance hearing and speaking. Healing appears to be beyond me."

"I heard a rumor you're taking your wielding seriously, Louis," Dain said.

Louis shrugged. "A bit."

Regan rolled his eyes. "He's fond of his new trick. He can go invisible. Something to do with using air to bend light or other such nonsense. In any case, he goes invisible. He likes to sneak up and scare people and do mischievous things."

"Damn right I do," he said with a grin.

Sylvane's eyes widened in shock. "Such language," she admonished.

The group spoke for a few minutes after their desserts were cleared away when the carriage back to the Academy was announced. Lora curtsied to Regan. "Thank you for your hospitality, Prince Regan. Good to see you, Master Dain. It was a pleasure, Master Geoffrey." Her mouth twitched when she got to Sylvane. "Thank you, your highness." She wasn't sure what to say, since any compliment would be insincere and way too hard to vocalize. She looked to Louis who was just accepting a glass of brandy from a servant. "You're not coming?"

"Nope," said swirling it in his glass. "Brandies with the boys."

Lora frowned. If brandy tasted as bad as it smelled, she was glad not to be invited to stay. She was not keen on going back alone though, even with the prince's private carriage. "I will see you tomorrow then, Master Louis." She curtsied to the room and followed a servant out to the carriage.

CHAPTER 24

Sylvane turned sixteen a few days after the fall term resumed. She piled her hair on her head and wore her corset during all of her classes. Not to be outdone, the other girls followed suit as they could. Catty's nut brown tresses knew no bounds, whether it be bun, pompadour, braided upsweep, twist, or whatever she could dream up and Genea, who had the deftest fingers, could produce. As Genea and Lora could not wear their hair up, their focus was on tying their corsets tighter than Sylvane and wearing their hair as high as they dared.

The boys thought they were absolutely ridiculous, but they admired the effects all the same.

"Isn't it a huge waste of time for you to put on that getup only to take it off every afternoon?" Peter gestured to Genea's abnormally small waistline. "Same with the hair."

The girls rolled their eyes. "As a wielder, I don't change every day after lunch," Genea explained gently. "But if you think on it, I mean think really hard, you might realize that every woman takes off this getup every evening before bed." She shook her head. "Same with the hair."

Peter's color rose. "Still seems like a waste of time," he muttered. "Plus, the swordsplayers put it all back on for dinner again. Twice in one day. That stuff is not easy to get off and put back on."

Catty grinned wickedly. "It's not?"

"No, it's not," Peter replied, oblivious to the gleam in Catty's eye and the warning glances from the other young men.

"Spend a lot of time getting into women's bodices and under their skirts then, Peter?" Catty shook her head and tsk'ed. "Shocking. What would your mother say?"

Peter flushed even redder. "I never pretended to be a monk," he sheepishly said after a moment.

The group teased Peter unmercifully about his conquests, of which he would divulge no additional information, for the entire term. He was good natured about it, since he'd walked right into the trap in the first place. But he was much choosier about his wording after that.

Midterm, Regan made his apologies to Genea as he handed invitations out to everyone else for the midwinter ball at the palace. Genea took being left out in stride and just shrugged. "Your sister will invite me next year," she said. "You're not my only in to the palace, you know. And in the odd event she and I have a falling out, being your cousin, it will be difficult to avoid coming whether I want to or not."

"Why wouldn't Regan invite you himself next year?" Lora felt sure she was missing something.

Regan nodded. "I'll be nineteen this spring, so I'll be sent out on assignment next fall. More than likely," he yawned, "being sent out will just mean being sent to work in the palace where my father and his advisors can still keep an eye on me. So I'll still be around—and with more freedom to cause havoc."

"Surely the Academy and your father both know you need more experience than you can get at home?" Catty asked, her voice heavy with indignance.

"I'm sure they do," Regan agreed. "Having me *assigned* to the palace makes them feel better about it, I guess."

Lora had just begin to understand what exactly went on during these assignments. Dain and she had started up their correspondence again since the new year, and he was full of stories about what he had been doing at James Lake. And it wasn't just avoiding or rolling his eyes at Geoff. He participated in council meetings, saw to the castle's defenses, and fought in border skirmishes. She wasn't sure what she had thought, but it certainly wasn't that he would be put in harm's way. James Lake was right on the border with Korlisse and anything could happen.

Dain had said after this summer, when he graduated from the Academy, he would be going home to Mount Rathbone, which was near the border with Erasteen. Relations with Erasteen were touchy as well, so he said being at James Lake was preparing him well to help his father and brother govern more effectively. Lora just didn't like to think of any of her friends in danger, and now that Regan would be nineteen, he'd be going off to fight too. Then it would be Peter and Louis, then Catty, and finally Genea, Sylvane, and herself.

Lora wondered where she would be assigned. Would it be near one of her friends? Would she be in a new place with no familiar faces? Would she fit in? Probably not, unless her friends were nearby. Would it be near her home? They usually didn't do that, except in Dain and Regan's cases. Would she get along with her hosts? Possibly. It was all so scary and uncertain.

She continued her discussions with Lord Cedric, even though she no longer needed the extra help. Lora found she liked talking with him and grew to think of him as she would her father. She began asking him "hypothetical" questions whenever she was struggling with life.

"I've been invited to the midwinter ball, Lord Cedric," Lora said.

Lord Cedric's head was bent over the chessboard. He had been teaching Lora. He said anyone with half her wit and intelligence needed to know how to play. "I'm sure you'll have a marvelous time, my dear."

Lora bit her lip. "I've never been to anything like it," she admitted. "I'm afraid I'll say or do something stupid, and I'll never be able to show my face again."

"Nonsense," he said, still continuing to set up the board. Lord Cedric always placed each piece with care. "Your friends will be there. You have a dress being made for the occasion—I've heard you talking with Miss Catherine about it. You've learned all the dances and protocol as well as any other student, if Mistress Diane is to be trusted in assessing you, which she is."

"I'm nervous."

The old man looked up from the chess board. "You've talked with your friends about this?" When she shook her head, he sighed. "Lora, you're a lovely young woman. You are intelligent and will be able to carry on a meaningful conversation with anyone you come across. You will have dance partners. More than you would like, I expect. Young men talk, you know." He shook his head. "You will enjoy yourself. Don't look upon this as yet another challenge. It's a time for merrymaking and fun. Remember that." He gestured to Lora. He had put the white pieces in front of her.

She smiled and carefully chose her pawn. "Thank you," she told him. She had needed the type of reassurance her father would give her and couldn't.

"Not at all," he replied, charging into play with his knight. "I know you are not able to speak with your family on a regular basis. In fact, I've never heard you speaking of your father and older brother's correspondence. I assume that Lord Allistair and Lady Tiana just carry messages for them?"

Lora nodded. She played another pawn. "Yes. They don't write to me."

Lord Cedric paused, lost in thought. He moved a pawn and sat back in his chair. "Not all commoners can read and write," he said after a while.

"Oh they can read and write," she replied. She reached for another pawn and stopped, her hand hovering over it. Tears filled her eyes. She sat back and put her hands in her lap. She took the handkerchief her offered her and sniffed. "How did you know?"

"I've always known," he said. "Lord Allistair's mother was my sister. I've been to Haven Dale more times than I can count. Before you arrived at the Academy, I'd never seen or heard of you, so I was immediately suspicious. I started poking about and got in touch with the reeve of your village. Nice fellow. Told me all about Mark Fletcher and his family. A son and a daughter. The son was following in his father's footsteps as a fletcher. He wasn't sure about the daughter though, as she'd been sent away when she was twelve. Explains your predilection toward archery, my dear."

Lora bit her lip. "Are they kicking me out? Am I being thrown into prison for lying about this for so long?"

Lord Cedric laughed. "I've not told anyone. You can do that yourself when you're ready. And your place in society is assured because you are a swordwielder. You are not what you once were. Now, make your move."

Her heart wasn't in the game, so Lora quickly lost. She made her apologies to Lord Cedric and escaped as quickly as she could to mull things over. *How many other people had guessed?* she wondered.

Over the next few days, she overanalyzed every interaction she had with her friends, acquaintances, and her teachers. Lord Robert got so cross with her that he bound her arms in place with air so that she could not move and then dumped a large amount of water on her that he had gathered from the nearby air. Lord Michael refused to conjure up fire to help dry her off, and instead threatened to dump earth on her so that she became a muddy mess.

After that, Lora kept her brooding to mealtimes, study time, and bedtime. Her friends were used to such behavior from her from time to time and left her alone for the most part.

Regan did not. "Look alive, Haven Dale," he sat as he slid into the chair across from her in the library. "I'm tired of having you only half present at dinner. It isn't dignified, you know. And it won't do at the ball." He gave her a meaningful look. "The winter holidays are nearly upon us. You haven't forgotten, I trust."

Lora scowled. "How could I forget? Catty drags me to Mistress Bethany's nearly every day for fittings, as if anything changes in a day."

"Ah, yes," he steepled his hands in front of him. "The dress. Catty chatters on about the dresses nonstop. Festive red and green, I'm told?"

Her scowl deepened. "I'd rather not talk about it," she muttered and pulled her book on Erastinian diplomacy closer to her only to half-shout, "Hey!" when Regan slid it away. A nearby librarian shushed her and gave them a punitive look.

"You don't want to come." He was not asking a question.

"It's not that simple," she told him futilely reaching for her book.

Regan raised an eyebrow. "No? And here I thought you either wanted to come or you didn't. If I'd realized you were so reticent, I'd have skipped sending you an invitation."

"We've had this conversation before, Regan," she sighed. "Many times. I've argued the point with Catty, as well. And probably Dain. And most recently, Lord Cedric in a way."

"That's a lot of arguing," Regan said, still holding the book hostage. "You'd think that you would take the opinions of at least three friends and a teacher you admire into account." A mischievous gleam appeared in his eye. "Or perhaps I'll need to give you a title just to quiet your grumbling."

Lora stared down at her hands, resigned. "I always knew my place before I came here," she said, her voice barely above a whisper. "My path was laid out in front of me. Straight as day. Everything changed when I came here, and I am having trouble finding my place, even after four years. I am laughed at when I say I'll just go back to my old life after graduation. I'm scoffed at if I appear to believe I'll do more. So, what do I believe? The words of my kind and well-meaning friends? The few words of my often harsh but very pragmatic cousins? What say you, your highness?" She crossed her arms in front of her chest and scowled again.

Regan rolled his eyes. "There's no reasoning with you, but you have to realize, not everything is black and white like you seem to think." He pushed back his chair, stood up, pushed his hair out of his eyes, and patted her on the head. "I'll leave you to your obviously fascinating reading on the failure of diplomacy between Ydris and Erasteen. Yes, that's how it ends, so I can spare you the tedium." He gave her a little mocking bow and strode away.

The following day, Lora found herself on a pedestal in Mistress Bethany's shop with Catty lolling on a chaise nearby. "Am I really being so stupid?" she asked as Mistress Bethany pinned and repinned the stubborn silk. Lora winced as the pin's point grazed her skin.

"You're rarely stupid," Catty told her as she popped a caramel into her mouth.

"You know what I mean," Lora told her as she raised her arm for Mistress Bethany. "Am I stupid for being fitted for a dress I might never wear the likes of again? Am I stupid for thinking I might never wear the likes of it again? Am I just stupid in general?"

Mistress Bethany chuckled. "I had a young man in here asking about you the other day, my dear. He was no pauper, I assure you. Regardless of whatever you think your position is, others have always been willing to overlook it. You are marvelous as you. No strings attached. No titles or large fortune needed." She paused. "Those are always helpful, but there are a lot of empty-headed souls or cruel sorts who have one or both. It doesn't do them one bit of good." She lowered Lora's arm and raised the other. "Did I hit the nail on the head, then?"

Catty laughed as well as she could with a mouth full of caramel. "That's what we've been trying to tell her for four years now. She fears setting her sights too high only to have what's real come crashing down on her, I think. It's too bad she won't be convinced that those who'd let anything crash down aren't worthy of her notice."

"When are you sixteen, my dear?" Mistress Bethany lowered Lora's arm and walked around her, frowning.

"In just over a sevenday," she said. She couldn't sigh because her laces were so tight.

"And already you've given yourself indigestion over this matter?" Mistress Bethany clucked her tongue, and smoothed out a seam. "Do you have some ogre of a mother, aunt, or grandmother— or cousin—hovering over you demanding you get married at the earliest moment possible? There are young ladies who would kill to be in your position, you know. You have very important skills that are held in higher regard than your ability to produce heirs, you know."

Catty giggled. "And you know you don't have to be titled, rich, or married to have fun at a ball!" She had finally gotten her teeth apart and was sipping on a glass of water.

Lora looked skyward. "Fine!" she conceded. "Can we please talk about something else now?"

"Excellent!" Catty sat right up. She waggled her eyebrows. "Pregnancy potions, then?"

Lora's cheeks flamed crimson and Mistress Bethany laughed. "I make a strong one if you have the need, Miss Lorana," the tailor said as she started to calm down.

"I most certainly do not have the need," Lora declared.

"No? Well, you might. I hear that Geoffrey of James Lake has done nothing but pester our handsome prince about you since you met this summer," Catty put in.

"He's a clod," Lora declared. "Besides, I don't like anyone. No one has kissed me, so I really don't think I'll skip that step and head straight on into pregnancy potion territory." She nodded to the tailor. "I appreciate the thought though. Someday, I may want some and am glad to know where I can find it."

Catty squealed. "No kisses?" She swooned onto the chaise. "What about Peter?"

Lora rolled her eyes. "Peter is like my brother. He'd just as soon break my nose again as kiss me. And don't ask about anyone else. My answers will be much the same."

"I guess we'll just have to expand your social circle," Catty teased.

Too soon for Lora's comfort, her birthday arrived. One day until the dreaded ball. The gown hung in her room, a terrible and constant reminder of what was to come. All of her friends had stayed over the holiday due to their invitations to the midwinter ball at the palace. Regan and Sylvane were, of course, at the palace, and Genea was at her family's home. Peter, Louis, and Catty stayed at the Academy, of course.

Shortly after the sun rose, there was a knock at Lora's door. She undid the air bindings and opened the door only to be tackled by Genea and Catty. "Happy birthday!" they chorused.

Lora rolled her eyes. "Thank you," she said. "I'm half starved. Perhaps we could take these celebrations to the dining hall?"

Genea shook her head. "No more going out without your laces drawn. Oh the scandal!"

"I figured as much," Lora grumbled.

She gestured for her friend to turn around. And she helped her finish getting properly dressed. Genea nodded. "Now, we can head out," she said. "No more starving for the birthday girl."

Catty giggled, and Genea and she each took an arm and towed their unwilling friend with them to breakfast. Lord Cedric nodded at her and winked from over his steaming mug of tea. Mistresses Tabitha, Diane, and Flora came by and kissed her on the cheek, much to her embarrassment. And Lord Michael and Lord Robert raised their steaming mugs to her over their meals.

"This is so embarrassing," Lora complained as they found a table. "No one ever said or did anything on my other birthdays."

"This isn't like any other birthday," Catty told her. "You'll be viewed in a whole new light. Things you could get away with yesterday, you won't be able to today. You'll also be getting different sorts of attention than you're used to."

Louis and Peter slid into the seats across from them. "Did we miss anything?" Louis asked. "I'm starved."

Peter slid a small package toward Lora. "I know you don't do gifts, but here you are. It's from Louis and me," he said. He grinned and served himself some hotcakes and sausage.

When Lora opened her mouth to complain, Genea cut her off and slid another gift in front of her. "Don't start," she said, scolding her. "Just accept them. You're our friend. We don't care about anything else." She placed the pastries they all knew Lora liked on her friend's plate and added a few strips of bacon.

Catty signaled for some tea. "That one is from Genea and me."

"I wanted to get you something useful, like garters—hey!" Louis put his hand over his reddening cheek before a smack sounded several inches in front of his face. "Two can play at that game!"

"You're so vulgar, Louis," Lora said, shaking her head. "And you can't complain about the air slap. I got you fair and square. You're faster than I am with your shield." She gestured to the unmarked side of his face. "You got it there before I could." She grinned and began untying the knot and the gift from Peter and him. "Ooh! Chocolate turtles! This is much better than a garter. Far more useful. I can't eat a garter, after all."

Genea nudged her. "No talk of garters, not even when you're goaded by that imbecile over there." She pointed at Louis and frowned. "You're an adult."

Lora blushed, set her candy down, and picked up the gift from the girls. Inside was a pair of delicate silver earrings. "These are lovely," she said. "They're perfect for tomorrow."

"Oh, we know," Catty teased. "I've been at all of your fittings, after all."

She rolled her eyes and took a bite of the pastry Genea had so thoughtfully placed on her plate. Lora had had friends in Haven Dale, but nothing like this. She considered herself a very lucky young woman—there, she admitted it. A very lucky young woman, indeed.

CHAPTER 25

The day of the ball dawned bright and clear. Freezing, but bright and clear. The little bit of snow that had fallen before midwinter was crusty and icy. The cobbled streets and paths were slick with ice. Multitudes of workers were out before dawn salting everything down so that no person or horse would be injured in a fall.

The friends had stayed up late the night before so they would be assured to sleep late. Sleeping late on a day when you knew you'd be up all night was as important a part of the preparation as anything else. As a result, Lora woke up early, tired, and cross.

Woman or not, she was not about to bother either of her friends to help get her dressed that morning, so she decided to forgo her corset. Until she ran into Mistress Tabitha who turned her around and saw her properly dressed for breakfast. Lora sighed and walked to the dining hall silent and alone.

She served herself up some fried bread and jam, signaled for a mug of hot cider, and dug into her breakfast. The normally tasty meal was dry and tasteless on her tongue. She forced herself to eat, since she knew it would likely be the only time she could choke anything down. When she was finished, Lora went straight to the bath and soaked for as long as she dared. She had high hopes the warm water would calm her nerves and allow her to nap for a few hours, as Catty had done the previous year.

When she had soaked her fill, Lora quickly made her way back to her room. She found the pacing duo of Catty and Genea waiting for her outside her room. "Where have you been?" they chorused.

"I woke up early," Lora replied as she released the air binding on her door. She was glad to have it. It helped avoid awkward surprises. "So I went and had breakfast and took a bath." She gave them a very significant look. "I had hoped the bath would calm me down enough so that I could nap."

Catty laughed. "You thought you could nap on this momentous occasion?"

Lora rolled her eyes. "Yes. You napped last year on this momentous occasion, so it wasn't such a huge stretch of my imagination."

"If you insist," Genea said with a curtsy. "We'll leave you alone. But I have to warn you that it's nearly noon. I guess your bath took longer than you thought?" She nodded at Lora's grimace. "You'll only have a couple of hours to sleep and get awake. Then it's beautification time." She sighed. "I wish I were going. My parents are stricter than yours, Catty. They won't let me go even though I'm older now than you were last year." Catty blushed prettily.

"Well, I guess I'd better get back to resting," Lora said changing the subject to what it was before Genea's awkward tangent. "Shall I come find you when I wake?"

"No, we'll come to you," Catty said. "That way we know you'll have enough time." She squealed. "Oh, I'm so excited!"

Try though she might, Lora could not fall asleep. Her mind raced. Would she have fun? Would they think her crude and crass?

Would they know she was common? Would she make a fool of herself? Who would she dance with? Would anyone dance with her at all? Would she drink too much? Would she spill her food or drink? Would she trip on her gown? Would her corset be so tight that she popped out of it, ripping her dress to shreds? How many times would she try and slap Louis for making lewd comments about everything in a skirt including, it would seem, her?

She didn't sleep, that much was certain. She did not even think she had rested. Lora did not want to think about how that would make her feel after midnight. If she even made it that far. She stretched her arms above her head and simply waited for her friends to knock. She did not end up waiting for very long.

Lora was dragged through the older students' dorm suites by Catty and Genea to Mistress Tabitha's suite. The housemistress for the female swordsplayers welcomed them into her rooms so that the two older girls could change together. Catty had made her promise that she would give her opinion on how they looked and give advice on how best hair and accessories were to be arranged.

Genea took the underthings Mistress Bethany had made especially for this occasion and giggled as she laid them out. "A silk chemise and stockings? Trimmed with lace? Remind me to forgo the ball next year," she said in between gasps. "Call me boring, but I'll take my plain winter flannels, thank you very much."

Lora shimmied out of her dress and underthings and quickly took the undergarments Genea thought were so amusing from Mistress Tabitha's ladies maid. Mistress Tabitha had thought they could use more help and had asked her to join them. She pulled on her stockings and fastened them to her garters and fastened on her corset. The corset, like the underthings, was made specifically to be worn under a low cut, off the shoulder evening gown. Even with these on, Lora still felt naked.

Lindsey, the ladies maid, guided Lora off to Mistress Tabitha's bed post so she could hold onto it while her laces were being drawn. "I hope you have an idea on how far you need to go," she told the maid. "All I know is that even though it was as tight as it could possibly go during my fittings, Mistress Bethany said she was making it even tighter for tonight."

"Of course, miss," Lindsey said as she gestured for Lora to turn around. Having someone she shared a rank with call her something deferential made Lora feel strange. But she had promised Mistress Bethany she would try, so try she would.

The ladies maid was true to her word and pulled on Lora's laces for all she was worth. Lora walked around for a few moments afterward to get used to the tighter fit while Catty was getting squeezed into her smaller shape. Mistress Tabitha then held out the first of many petticoats that were to go under the dress so that Lora could step into them.

The putting on of underthings went on for several more minutes until Lindsey snapped her fingers and held up a brush. Lora and Catty each sat on a stool while the three other women contemplated the best way to do up their hair. A curling iron was hung over the coals and would evidently be used for each of them.

Genea began braiding Lora's hair along the temples and secured it back with pins when she reached the crown of her head. Masses of semi-mousey brown, semi-golden brown hair were piled in a complex up do. A few tendrils were left down and curled. Catty's nut brown hair was twisted up by Lindsey and had spiral curls cascading down her back. Neither girl, it was decided, needed hair adornments.

Lindsey then held Lora's dress out for her to step into. With as deep a breath as she could manage, Lora resolutely stepped in. The ladies maid walked around her and deftly did up the back. It fit perfectly, of course. Lindsey walked around and did up a couple of hooks in the front and then finally seemed satisfied.

"I'd meant to ask Mistress Bethany what the front fastenings were for, but I kept forgetting," Lora remarked.

Mistress Tabitha smiled coyly. "Officially, they're for opening up the dress and corset in the event you should faint. Unofficially, they're for wandering hands." She gave Lora a wink.

Lora blushed furiously and Catty laughed. She looked radiant in a gold trimmed burgundy gown. The sleeves were lightly puffed and came just up to the top of the shoulder. The sweetheart neckline dipped low, but not so low that it was improper for an unmarried woman to be wearing it. Genea placed a necklace of gold around Catty's neck, fastened some gold earbobs into her lobes, and pronounced her complete.

Lindsey placed the necklace Lora's mystery benefactor had given her the year before around her neck and fastened on the new silver filigreed earrings that Catty and Genea had given her the day before. The lady's maid led her to Mistress Tabitha's large mirror and stepped to the side.

Standing there where she expected herself to be was a young woman. A stranger with her face. Lora's dress was such a dark shade of green as to be nearly black. Tiny bits of silver lace and trim adorned it. The neckline began at the tips of her shoulders and sloped down gently in a v, which stopped just above where her cleavage began. It made Lora flush to know that Mistress Bethany had made the dress show absolutely as much as it could without being inappropriate to her age. The sleeves were tight from the tips of her shoulders down to her elbows where they ruffled gently to spill over the joint. The necklace and earrings could not have matched more perfectly. Even her hair had a more golden sheen to it, instead of its usual muddy brown.

"Such lovely girls we have here at the Academy," Mistress Tabitha said with a smile. "Lovely ladies with deadly skills. Perhaps that's what we should tell the families of the young women who want to come here, but aren't allowed. You still retain oodles of femininity."

Catty rolled her eyes. "It's all those etiquette lessons. I think Master Franklin beats womanliness into us with the staff he uses to keep time while we all dance." She shook her head and spun around, a smile lighting her face as she came forward again. "Is Regan's carriage here yet, I wonder?" Lindsey held out a fur-trimmed cloak for her and she quickly put it on.

"It arrived a few moments ago," Genea said. "I slipped out while Lora was admiring herself. No, no. No blushing, Miss Lorana of Haven Dale." She grinned at her friends. "Now get along with you. The ball awaits!"

Lora walked forward and kissed the three ladies who had been so instrumental in getting them to where they were on their cheeks. Catty did the same and then led Lora out of the room by the arm before she had the opportunity to run.

"I can't believe I let you talk me into this," Lora murmured. "Nothing good will come of it."

Catty rolled her eyes. "You look amazing—*we* look amazing! Sylvane will look like she's swallowed a bug all night because of how amazing you and I look. Our friends—*and more* will ask us to dance. We'll eat and we'll drink sparkling white wine." She paused. "So what if there are whispers. So what if we spill something or laugh too loudly. It's a ball. Worse things will have happened."

The two of them stepped out into a winter wonderland. The tops of all the buildings were crowned with puffy white snow. The roads were dusted with a thin film of powdery whiteness with no sinister gleams of ice beneath. The air was crisp and clear. There was no wind. No snow fell. It was perfect. Lora took a deep breath and accepted it. She accepted the night for what it was. A royal ball. An opportunity to have fun. If it was a unique experience in her life, she would have to know in her heart that she had made the most of it.

A footman held a hand out to her in front of the carriage Prince Regan had made available for them that evening. Lora placed her hand in his and looked back at Catty as she stepped up into the carriage. She smiled, finally allowing her feelings of dread to fade into feelings of excitement and anticipation. She smiled and said, "Let's go."

Catty squealed and nearly bowled the footman over in her eagerness to get into the carriage and to the palace. "Absolutely!" She grinned and settled into her seat.

The night was just beginning.

To Larry, for asking for more and inspiring me to finish this one in the first place.

To Colin, always.

To Maryrose, for this and From Embers. I bet you and Jon never thought you'd be acknowledged in books for your much appreciated help!

To the boys, I know I've tested your patience. Thanks for always giving me hugs and kisses when I asked for them. Writing is a gut-wrenching labor of love, and you guys lifted me up more than you know.

To my readers. I know I'm putting you last on this one, and for that, I'm sorry. I never thought that people would really want to read my books—let alone buy them! You have overwhelmed and humbled me. I cannot thank you enough! Next time, you sure as heck won't be last!!

Andrea Irving has been writing for practically her whole life. She started off in her own little fantasy worlds, but has been spending much of her recent time having nightmares while writing YA horror. She is happy to be bringing YA fantasy back into her repertoire. A physician and college professor by day, her previous publications were purely scientific. She is very happy to finally be sharing her more creative works with the world. Andrea lives and works in the Phoenix, AZ area with her husband and two sons.